Th
Cottage
on
Wildflower
Lane

LIZ DAVIES

Published by Lilac Tree Books

CHAPTER 1

Bored. Bored, bored, bored. Had she mentioned that she was bored? Dear God, if something didn't happen soon, she was going to be forced to liven things up by doing something drastic, such as stripping down to her knickers and running around the office wearing nothing else except her shoes and her ID badge.

Esther had a horrible feeling no one would notice.

She tapped out a rhythm on the desk using her pen. 'Guess this tune,' she said to the office in general, but didn't have any takers.

Now there was a surprise. Not.

Please ring, please, she begged silently, giving the phone a pleading look. It ignored her too.

What on earth was she doing here? There clearly wasn't enough work for the permanent staff, so she had no idea why the bank felt the need to employ a temp such as her. On the plus side, the work was hardly rocket science. Booking account managers in for appointments with clients didn't take much in the way of intelligence, and neither did the subsequent working out of the commission from any sales those managers achieved. Esther ran six managers; she could easily have handled double that. Treble, even.

She'd been working there for three weeks now. When she first started she'd offered to take on additional jobs and asked if she could help anyone but she'd been soundly put in her place. After that, she'd begun to wonder if she was missing something vital, that perhaps she should be doing something that she wasn't.

Now though, she realised that the meagre amount of work she was doing was all that was actually expected of her.

She studied the girl sitting to her right. Glossy hair caught up in a sophisticated bun, glasses perched on the end of her nose, immaculate make-up, nails so long they could take an eye out at fifty feet, and sexy secretary clothes. In other words, a pencil skirt, sheer blouse, and a pair of scarily high stilettos. Esther felt positively frumpy in comparison, despite wearing a new suit (trousers, of course), and a decent heel for a change.

She continued to stare at Clara, who was always

busy, despite doing exactly the same job as Esther. She wondered what it was that kept her colleague's attention so firmly on her computer screen. The only things of interest on Esther's screen were Rightmove (which would be great if she intended to move house), several games (the bank obviously *expected* their employees to waste time) and Google maps. Actually, those were the only sites which the company allowed her access to. The rest of the stuff was work-related and as boring as watching paint dry.

By the end of her first week, courtesy of Google Street Maps and 3D, Esther knew her way around Southern Australia better than her commute to work. The added bonus for the map-thing was that it gave her information about each place. Today she decided that Milan should have her attention. She'd always fancied Milan, mainly because of the clothes and shoes but also because it was Italy, the land of romance and dark-haired, stubble-sporting, chocolate-eyed Italian men, hopefully with a better fashion sense than Josh.

Sorry, Josh, she immediately thought, feeling guilty at being disloyal to her boyfriend but bless him he did have a liking for loud shirts and shiny pointy shoes.

Esther delved into the handbag by her feet and surreptitiously checked her phone for messages. Nothing.

With a sigh, she slipped it back inside. Employees weren't supposed to use their mobiles whilst at work, and it was frowned upon to even have them on. Something to do with a security risk apparently, although Esther couldn't quite figure out what. If she wanted to make a note of someone's account details (not that she ever would, but there were some genuinely dodgy people about) she could do it just as effectively with pen and paper. But the bank was quite happy for its minions to shuffle copious amounts of A4 and assorted forms around, normally from one desk to another with little in the way of obvious results.

Speaking of desks, Sally wasn't at hers yet. Sally sat opposite her, separated by a computer screen and a selection of stationery which was lined up neatly and in some kind of order that she had yet to work out.

Thankfully, she had no one on her right as her own desk was tight up against the window. The view was of rooftops and the upper stories of an assortment of other city buildings, but at least she could see outside. Sometimes she caught sight of a bird. Two, if she was lucky.

She checked her watch, wondering where Sally could be. It was her colleague's turn to make the coffee and Esther was gasping. She could always go and make one anyway, but the last time she'd done so she'd been soundly scolded for messing up the rota, even though she'd offered to make the coffee run a permanent thing.

9.25 a.m. Was that all it was? She could have sworn it was at least mid-morning. It felt like she'd put in a good three-hour shift already, but she'd only been here thirty minutes.

She risked a swift peek at her phone again, dying to give Facebook a quick scroll, when a chorus of "good mornings" broke the monotony.

Sally had arrived.

This was another lady who was always immaculately dressed and groomed, except she was short, blond, and somewhere in her late-fifties, compared to Clara's tall, chestnut and mid-twenties.

'Apologies, people, but I had to book a cruise,' the older woman announced as she waltzed into the office.

Nice for some, Esther thought with a hint of envy. Apparently Sally hadn't long had a holiday, and now here she was booking another. Esther hadn't even been on one this year yet. But she *was* hoping. Josh had taken an inordinate amount of interest in Spain recently, ever since he'd come back from that stag weekend which he'd been on a couple of months ago, and she hoped he was planning a surprise holiday for them both. It was ages since they'd been away together.

Last year they'd only managed a weekend in West Wales and a few days in Devon, because Josh had gone on a boys' holiday to Malaga and couldn't afford anything else.

Esther was desperate for a bit of sun on her face. The summer was already half over and so far the British weather was living up to its reputation. It hadn't stopped raining for weeks.

Esther blamed the schools. As soon as the children broke up for the summer holidays, the heavens opened and it didn't stop raining until they went back in September.

'Where are you off to this time?' Clara asked.

Sally applied more lipstick before she answered, and Esther watched in fascination as the older woman swiped a fresh coat of colour across her lips without using a mirror. If she tried that, she'd end up looking like Coco the Clown.

'Only around the Med, starting at Palma in Majorca and finishing in Crete.'

Esther couldn't believe how matter-of-fact Sally was. If she'd just gone and booked a cruise, she simply knew she'd be bouncing off the walls with excitement.

The break in monotony that Sally's late arrival caused lasted all of fifteen minutes, and that included the riveting task of making the coffee. Then it was back to exploring Milan and hoping the phone would ring.

Once again she wondered if she wasn't doing something that everyone else was. It would explain why the rest of the support staff (five of them, not including her) were all so busy and why she wasn't. The office could accommodate double their number but was barely half full today. Another row of desks was set at right angles to hers, situated in the middle of the room, but none of those workstations were occupied right now. They were reserved for the account managers to use when they needed to. Clearly none of them needed to use their desks today, so the office was unusually quiet.

Her phone rang, making her jump.

'Private Banking, how may I help you?' she sang.

'It's Liam. Book Mr and Mrs Gore in for Monday next week, ten-thirty, please. Mark it down as an ISA.'

'Okay,' Esther replied, tapping away. 'All booked. Anything else I can do for you?'

'No thanks, doll, you're a star.'

Esther was left holding a dead phone and wondering why the account managers couldn't use the iPads they'd all been issued with to do their own bookings. It would cut out the middle-man (in other words, her).

On second thoughts, they could phone every five minutes if it meant her keeping this job. It might only be a temporary position, but the bank wanted her until Christmas and although she might be bored this was a damned sight easier than many of the places she'd been sent to by the agency.

Liam rang again. 'Just a thought, what are you doing after work?'

Oh my, she hadn't been expecting that. She was so new here that he probably didn't realise she was in a relationship. 'Actually, I've got a boyfriend,' she said, feeling quite flattered he'd asked. Liam was rather dishy in a brash, over-confident way.

'Fab. Bring him along,' he said.

'Excuse me?' Esther's eyes nearly popped out of her head at the suggestion.

'We're all meeting at Chester's after work. Pass the word on, would ya?'

'Oh. Of course. Right. I'll do that. Thanks.'

She felt like a right idiot, and he probably thought that she was a weirdo now. With too-hot cheeks, she answered a third call. Blimey, she was in demand this morning. Three calls in less than fifteen minutes? Things were beginning to look up.

But it wasn't Liam, nor was it any of the account managers, and her heart did its usual little flip when she heard the voice on the other end. She and Josh had been together for two years and he still made her go weak at the knees on occasion.

'Hiya babes, I'm so glad you called,' she murmured, trying to keep her voice low so the wagging ears around her couldn't overhear that she was on a personal call. 'I'm bored out of my skull. How's work?'

Josh was a delivery driver and the tales he could tell about the sights he saw on his rounds often had her in stitches.

'Okay, I suppose. That's why I rang.'

Something in his tone sounded a bit off, and a vague prickle of unease ran down her spine.

'What's up, Josh? You haven't had an accident, have you? Please say you aren't hurt.'

'No, I'm fine. Listen, I've got something to tell you and you aren't going to like it.'

Esther guessed what was coming. Josh had been making noises about jacking his job in and going to work for his mate, Andy, who owned a pub or a wine bar. She wasn't quite sure exactly what it was, or where it was for that matter, because she hadn't really been listening. Josh was always threatening to change jobs, thinking that someone else's grass was greener than his own, but he hadn't done anything about it so far.

'I'm going to work for Andy,' he announced.

'Good. You won't be travelling miles every day,' she said. 'You know how much I worry about all the driving you do. Do you fancy going out later to celebrate? A group of people from work are going to Chester's.'

'I can't. I told you, I'm going to work for Andy.'

'What? So soon? I hope you don't have to work every evening.' They'd never get to see each other if that was the case, and it would be a definite downside to working behind a bar. 'What's that noise?' she asked, before he had a chance to reply. It sounded like the bing-bong you get in a railway station when they make an announcement, and she felt another little shiver of unease.

'I'm at the airport.'

'Which one?' she asked, wondering where he was delivering to today. Worcester was roughly halfway between Bristol airport and Birmingham, so he could be in either.

'Does it matter?'

No, she didn't suppose it did, but his round didn't usually take him so far afield. Maybe that was why he was going to work for this Andy guy – the company he worked for must have gone and changed his route again and he wasn't happy about it.

'Look babe, there's not much point in carrying on,' he was saying. 'I'll be over there and you'll still be here, and if it pans out then I'm not coming back for the winter. Andy says it's an all-year-round kinda place. It's a bit quieter in the winter like, but he says he'll keep me on anyway.'

'Excuse me?' Josh wasn't making sense. Why was he talking about the winter?

'The wine bar. He says I can stay all year. So I'm sorry, babe, but I'm calling it a day.'

Calling what a day? What did Josh mean? She caught Carla giving her a warning look out of the corner of her eye and she dimly registered that Dave, who ran their department plus two more, was on their floor, but she was too intent on trying to work out what Josh was saying to pay anything else much attention.

'I don't understand,' she said.

She heard his exasperated sigh. 'It's over, Esther. *We're* over. I'm off to Malaga and that's final.'

'Why Malaga?' she squeaked, confused and more than a little scared.

Another sigh. 'Because that's where the Pink Flamingo is.'

'What pink flamingo?' There must be something wrong with her ears, because Josh wasn't making any sense at all.

'Andy's bar, it's called the Pink Flamingo,' he huffed, and there was that bing-bong noise again, and

Esther felt like crying.

'I swear you never listen to a word I say. No wonder I—' Josh sighed again. 'Look, I've got to go, they've announced my flight. Take care of yourself, babe.'

And for the second time that morning, Esther was left holding a dead phone to her ear.

CHAPTER 2

Of course she tried calling him back – what else was she supposed to do? Ignoring the pointed looks from Sally and the curious glances coming from Clara's direction, she picked up the landline and dialled his number. At least she had the sense not to use her mobile with Dave in the room.

'Come on,' she muttered, tapping her nails on the desk as she waited for the call to connect.

It didn't.

It went straight to voicemail.

Josh must have switched his phone off.

Disbelief flooded through her in sickening waves. Had her boyfriend of two years just dumped her by phone?

Surely not; he couldn't have done. She must have heard him wrong, that's all.

Picking up her bag and getting to her feet, she

made her slightly wobbly way to the ladies' loos, conscious of several pairs of eyes watching her progress.

'I'm not used to heels,' she said chirpily, aiming her comment at the wall. Tears pricked at the back of her eyes and she blinked hard. There was no way on God's earth she was going to cry in front of this lot. Anyway, she probably didn't have anything to cry about because she'd simply misheard him. Malaga, indeed! He was probably sounding off about the stag weekend again. It was all he'd talked about for a while after he'd come back.

Her eyes narrowed. Not for the first time she wondered if he had been unfaithful while he was out there. She'd heard what could go on during those kind of weekends.

But no, not her Josh. He'd never cheat on her. The pair of them were like two little love birds cuddled up together in their nest. Their "nest" was actually a one-bedroomed flat above an off-licence on the outskirts of the city. It mightn't seem much, but it was theirs, their first home together. They were trying to save for a deposit to buy a place, but there seemed to be so much they needed to spend their money on that it was going to take them years to get on the property ladder – if they ever did.

Slamming in through the door of the ladies' toilets,

she headed straight for a cubicle, used a piece of tissue paper to protect her fingers as she closed the lid, then sat down.

She tried calling him, but yet again it went to answerphone.

Beginning to feel quite anxious now (there was a horrid fluttering sensation in her chest) she checked her Facebook account, scrolling through the posts ever more frantically to find the latest one from Josh.

She couldn't actually find him. He had disappeared from her feed, and when she checked, he was no longer in her friends' list either.

Nausea rolling in her stomach, she had a nasty suspicion she knew what had happened – he'd unfriended her.

Desperate to discover the truth, she put his name into the search bar. Josh Abbott.

Nothing.

She tried Joshua Abbott. Still nothing. Then Josh M Abbott, Joshua M Abbott, J M Abbott and every other variation she could think of.

Still nothing. Of course, there were loads of people named Josh Abbott out there, but none of them was *her* Josh.

She'd been blocked.

Twitter, she thought. He didn't use it often, but he had been known to post stuff on there now and again.

She couldn't find him on that site, either.

Slumping against the side of the cubicle, Esther let the tears fall.

He'd done it, he had actually dumped her!

What had he said? Something about Andy, Malaga, and a flamingo?

Wait, wasn't that the place he had been raving about when he'd come back from the stag weekend?

She was certain it was.

He couldn't possibly be going back to Spain. *Could he?*

With dread in her heart, she called his mum. She and Debbie hadn't hit it off from the start (Esther thought his mother babied him too much) but if anyone knew where Josh was and what was going on, Debbie would.

'It's me, Esther,' Esther announced, although Debbie would already know who it was from the number. 'How are you?' she added casually, not wanting to dive straight into the reason for her call, in case she had got the wrong end of the stick and Josh was sitting in his van somewhere on the A38 and cursing the traffic.

There was a pause on the other end, followed by a sigh. 'He's told you, then?'

'Told me what, Debbie?' Esther knew her voice

was too high and falsely bright, but she couldn't seem to help it. She was beginning to wish she hadn't phoned her boyfriend's mother at all.

'You wouldn't be ringing me if he hadn't,' Debbie stated flatly.

She had a point, Esther conceded. She never, ever rang Josh's mother unless it was absolutely necessary.

'It's true, then?' Even now, in the face of overwhelming evidence, she still didn't truly believe it. 'He's really gone to Spain?'

'It's true.'

'But why?' she wailed. 'I thought we were happy.'

'You might have been, but my Josh clearly wasn't or he wouldn't have gone.'

Thanks for pointing out the obvious and kicking a girl when she's down, Esther thought. 'Is he coming back? I mean, it's just for a week or two, right?'

'He told me it was for good. Now if you don't mind, I'm in the middle of having my roots done. I've gotta run. Oh, and before you go, I'll be around later to pick up the rest of his things. Bye.'

Esther was left staring at her phone yet again and wondering how her life had fallen apart in the space of half an hour.

CHAPTER 3

Was the end of a marriage ever easy? Kit wondered, as he stared at the letter from his wife's solicitor. Soon-to-be ex-wife, he should say. He wanted to do right by Nancy, he truly did, but asking – *demanding* – half of his share in the business he owned with his brother, was a step too far. He'd already agreed to sell the house and give her 50 per cent of the proceeds; the house that he'd bought with his own money he might add, and long before he'd fallen in love with Nancy. She had still been living with her parents, so it seemed logical for her to move in with him after they married.

In hindsight, it hadn't been logical at all, because she was now claiming half of everything he owned including the bloody car which, he'd pointed out, he needed for his job. Although, if her outrageous demands continued, he wouldn't have a job to need a car *for.*

He'd tried to keep their split amicable, despite everything, but now he felt the need to bring out the big guns and instruct his solicitor to fight her every inch of the way. Even if it cost him every penny he had, it was better than letting her get away with daylight robbery.

'Harvey? It's Kit Reynolds. I need your help.'

'Finally seen sense, have you?' his solicitor replied. 'Good. But it's not me you need to speak to. As I've told you before, I don't specialise in family law. I can recommend a good bloke, though. His name is Nash Layton. He's young, but don't let that fool you. He's got an excellent reputation. Works for Smith, Smythe and Crosby in Worcester. He'll either become a partner or set up his own firm shortly, mark my words.'

Kit grimaced. He wanted Harvey to handle his divorce. He knew Harvey, and Harvey knew him and his family. But he also realised that what the man said was true – he wasn't a divorce lawyer.

Harvey must have sensed his reluctance. 'Look, Kit, I know this isn't easy for you but from what you've told me, you need someone who specialises in this kind of thing.'

He sighed. 'Yeah, you're right. She's asking for half of my share of the business now, as well as half of the house.'

'I don't like to say it, but the starting point when it comes to division of assets is fifty-fifty. The court is able to apply an element of discretion as to the award given to each party, but unfortunately it won't discriminate between the homemaker and the breadwinner.'

'Nancy could work if she wanted to. It's not as though we've got any children which warrant her staying at home,' Kit protested. 'After we married, she jacked her job in so she could take some time out to have a think about what she wanted to do, but she decided she liked the lifestyle of being a lady who lunches. Luckily we could afford for her not to work.'

'Save it for Nash Layton,' Harvey advised. 'If you tell me the details you'll only get me all riled up and it's not good for my blood pressure.'

Despite his problems, Kit smiled fondly as they said their goodbyes, Harvey promising to contact this new man for him. Kit had a lot of regard for the elderly solicitor and respected his judgement. Nash Layton sounded like a firm of solicitors all by himself though, Kit thought. He would have preferred Harvey to handle this, but he realised the old lawyer didn't have the expertise. Harvey was roughly the same age as his parents and was probably due to retire soon, and he'd been advising the family ever since Kit could remember, so it was only natural he'd turn to him in his time of need. But Harvey's area of expertise was corporate law and he'd helped set up the legal side of the business which Kit and his brother owned between them. The solicitor knew what it meant to him, how they'd started with nothing but an idea, and had built it up into the thriving company it was today.

Now Nancy was threatening to destroy what he'd worked so hard for.

Once again his thoughts spiralled around in his mind. If he wasn't careful, he was in danger of losing both his business and his home. As it was, the house would definitely have to go – there was no way he could afford to buy her out and finance her share in LandScape Ltd at the same time.

An awful thought occurred to him; what if he couldn't raise enough money? Would that mean that his brother would own fifty per cent, and he and Nancy would own twenty-five per cent each? He shuddered. The idea of Nancy having a say in how the business was run made him go cold.

Their marriage was over. It had been over for more than a year before they'd officially separated if he was honest, but he'd continued to fight to keep it going long after it was clear it couldn't be resuscitated. They should have a clean break now, but if she owned a chunk of the company then they'd never be free of each other.

He'd better tell Dean what was going on. The sooner his brother knew about this, the better. Dean was the intellectual one, the level-headed one. He'd always been better at dealing with clients and people in general. Kit was the ideas guy, working more from intuition than rules and conventions. They made a good team, counter-balancing each other's strengths and weaknesses.

As Kit pulled into LandScape's sweeping drive, he thought of how their choices of living accommodation portrayed their different characters. Dean loved his apartment in the converted barn next to the company's offices, with its clean lines and modern interior, and his garden was the same, minimalist and ultra-modern. In contrast, Kit lived in an old cottage with a roof badly in need of rethatching and a typically English cottage garden which was currently a riot of colour and a haven for wildlife.

He didn't say a word as he strode into Dean's office, simply thrusting the letter at him and slumping down into a chair.

Dean read it, the colour fading from his face. 'She can't do this. Can she?'

'I hope not. Harvey is putting me in touch with some guy who specialises in this kind of thing. I'm going to fight her. I said I'd buy her out of the house, but as that's clearly not good enough for her...'

Dean opened his mouth to say something, but Kit shot him a warning look. There was nothing that his brother could possibly say now which hadn't already been said several times before. He knew he'd been a fool to marry Nancy but beating himself up over it wasn't going to change anything and it certainly wasn't going to help matters. He'd made his bed and he was simply going to have to lie in it. One thing was certain though, he'd be very careful the next time he gave his heart to anyone.

If, in fact, he ever did.

CHAPTER 4

Pizza and prosecco were usually a match made in heaven for Esther. That afternoon though, it had become more of a necessity, especially since the wine was taking a far greater hit than the food.

Unable to face going back into that office, she had phoned Dave from the safety of the women's toilets, telling him that she had a female-type emergency. This information, added to the fact that she'd informed him that she was calling him from the loo, was enough for him to hurriedly end the conversation with an awkward and embarrassed, 'I hope you feel better soon.'

Esther didn't care if she lost nearly a full day's pay. All she cared about was going home and seeing what, if anything, Josh had left behind.

Not much, as it turned out. All the new clothes he had bought for the stag weekend were gone, as were most of his shorts, T-shirts, and jeans. He'd left anything that was old or scruffy, and he'd also left his CD collection. Considering he only listened to music on his phone now, that wasn't a surprise. Knowing that Debbie would be true to her word and would turn up later to collect the rest of Josh's things, Esther grabbed a couple of plastic bags and stuffed everything of his that she could find inside. Then she carried them down to the front door and stacked them there. That way she wouldn't have to see Josh's mother and the smug self-satisfied look on her face. Debbie had never thought Esther was good enough for her precious son.

Back in her flat she took another long swallow of wine and eyed the cold pizza with distaste. Although, after she'd downed another bottle of the fizzy stuff she knew she'd be cramming it in her mouth with all the finesse of a two-year-old child who had got his hands on a family-sized bag of Haribo.

What was she supposed to do now, she wondered? One minute she was part of a couple, the next she was single, and her other half (ex other half) had buggered off to Spain to work in a bloody bar, of all things. She couldn't think what on earth had possessed him. He didn't know the first thing about bar work. The closest he'd ever come to pulling a pint was lifting a glass to his mouth. Mind you, the Pink

Flamingo didn't sound like the kind of place where many people would ask for pints. It sounded more like a cocktail and umbrella bar.

Esther narrowed her eyes, vaguely remembering him saying something about scantily clad girls dancing on one of the bars. Might it have been this Flamingo one? There was one way to find out, so she reached for her phone and searched for it. There were several Pink Flamingos but only one in Malaga, so she clicked on it and studied the page.

Her eyes narrowed even further.

Contact details, opening times, gallery, drinks menu – all the usual stuff. Then she saw something that made her sit up and rub her bleary, bloodshot eyes; there was a tab that said "webcam".

She took a deep breath. Did she really want to do this? Yes. Should she do it? No. But curiosity won over common sense and she clicked on the tab anyway.

To her dismay, it didn't appear to be working. There was a picture on the screen, but it wasn't moving. Either the damn thing was buffering (although she couldn't see the annoying little circle to indicate that it was) or something was wrong with it.

Hang on a second... she checked the time. It was only 2 p.m. (and she was halfway to being drunk already, to her shame), so maybe the bar wasn't open yet? Pleased with her powers of deduction she checked the opening times. Crikey, it didn't open until 9 p.m., but wait – someone had come into shot. It appeared the webcam worked, after all. She didn't know whether that was a good thing or a bad thing, because she suspected she might be watching it later this evening while sobbing into her cocoa.

Sod the cocoa, she was going to open the second bottle of wine. Not that she could remember finishing the first one, but she must have done because the bottle was empty and there was no one else in the flat except her. The realisation that she was on her own physically and emotionally, brought fresh tears to her eyes.

She was still sobbing when Charlie phoned.

'Hi, hon,' her friend said. 'I wasn't expecting you to answer, so I was going to leave you a voice message. Are you on your lunch break?'

'Not exactly,' Esther sniffed, swiping an arm across her face in lieu of a tissue.

'You don't sound at all well. Have you got one of those nasty summer colds? Is there anything I can do?'

Unless Charlotte could make Josh change his mind, then no, not really. Esther could do with some sympathy and a shoulder to cry on, though. 'Josh and I have split up,' she informed her hoarsely.

'Oh, hon, I'm so, so sorry. What did he do?'

Bless Charlie for assuming that Josh was at fault and that Esther had been the one to do the dumping. 'He's gone to work in a wine bar in Malaga, the selfish pig.'

'He's done *what*?'

'Malaga. The Pink Flamingo, it's called. Some guy by the name of Andy runs it.'

'When did this happen? You never said anything.'

'This morning. He rang me from the airport!'

'The git! That's low. I'm assuming you didn't know anything about it?'

'Not an inkling. It was a complete shock.'

'Where are you?' Charlie asked.

'At home. I told them I was ill because I couldn't face staying in work; I'd have gone out of my mind.'

'Right, I'll be along as soon as I finish my shift. I'll bring a bottle. No, two. And a takeaway. Love you, hon. Keep your chin up, yeah?'

Esther turned back to the screen as soon as the call ended. Some guy dressed in a pair of shorts and a bright orange Hawaiian shirt with blue parrots all over it was checking the vast assortment of bottles behind the bar.

It was the sort of shirt Josh had been favouring lately, but the guy wasn't him.

She hadn't honestly expected it to be. She had no

idea what time his flight was, where he was going to be staying, or even if he was expected to work tonight. Those opening hours should suit him down to the ground though, she thought. He never did like getting up in the mornings, so not going to bed until 5 or 6 a.m. wouldn't be a problem for him if it meant that he could stay in bed until midday.

Suddenly she wondered whose bed he would be sleeping in. Maybe this Andy fella was putting him up or had arranged accommodation for him. Or, maybe he'd met some girl while he was out there for that stag weekend and was going to move in with her. This morning, the thought of him cheating would never have occurred to her. But fewer than five hours later, she realised that nothing he did would surprise her.

If he was standing in front of her right now, she'd slap his face from here to next week.

Yeah, right, she said to herself – would this be before or after she begged him to come back?

Abruptly, a part of her hated him with the same degree of passion with which she had once loved him.

Oh, who was she kidding? *Had* loved him indeed? She still *did* love him, and to her dismay she couldn't see that changing any time soon.

CHAPTER 5

'Will you stop it!' Charlie said, trying to make a grab for Esther's phone. 'You've been staring at the damned thing all evening. You do know he's not going to phone or text, don't you?'

Esther knew. But she wasn't checking for missed calls or unnoticed texts. She was looking at the webcam. Constantly. She couldn't seem to stop herself. She was addicted to it already, which was probably quicker than someone getting hooked on hard drugs.

Despite the second bottle of wine that she'd drunk more or less all by herself, she and Charlie had also opened another one. Thank God Charlie had had the foresight to pick up a takeaway on the way over, or else Esther would probably be unconscious by now.

Maybe that wouldn't be such a bad thing, she mused drunkenly. At least being totally out of it would limit the time she would spend lying awake tonight and sobbing into her pillow.

Without warning, Charlie made another grab for her phone before Esther had a chance to react.

'Give it back!' she cried, but Charlie shook her head.

'I know you're grieving, Est, but you're going to ruin your eyesight if you keep staring at it. Oh!' Charlie's eyes widened and she slowly turned the screen around so Esther could see it. 'Is *this* what you've been doing? Looking at this? What is it?'

'A webcam.' Esther replied sheepishly.

'Why?' Charlie screwed up her eyes as she examined the screen. 'Oh, Esther, it's the bar that Josh has gone to work in, isn't it? The Pink Parrot.'

'Pink Flamingo,' she muttered.

'Whatever.' Charlie twisted in her chair to look at Esther's face straight on. 'You can't torture yourself in this way. It's not healthy.'

'Cut me some slack, will you? He only left me this morning. It's not as if I've been watching it for weeks, or even days.'

'But that's exactly what *is* going to happen,' Charlie predicted. 'You won't be able to help yourself. You'll turn into a cyberstalker.'

'No, I won't,' she objected. 'I just want to see him, that's all. One last time. I didn't get to say goodbye!'

she wailed.

'Yeah, the scumbag didn't even have the guts to tell you to your face.'

'It's because he doesn't like seeing me cry,' Esther said, defensively.

'If he wasn't such an arse you wouldn't need to cry,' Charlie pointed out. 'He was never good enough for you.'

Esther knew that wasn't true, but she appreciated the support all the same. Charlie, unlike ratbag Josh, could always be relied on to have her back. Charlie returned the phone to Esther and took her own mobile out of her pocket.

When her friend began scrolling down the screen, Esther felt a little put out. Charlie was supposed to be here for *her*, not to chat on Facebook or whatever it was she was doing. Esther picked up her wine glass, took a healthy gulp, and was about to say something when Charlie let out a little cry.

'What is it? What's wrong?' Esther wanted to know.

'I wanted to see if there are any more of those webcams out there and I've found loads. You know that place where Richard and I went on holiday last year, in Greece? You must remember? I didn't stop talking about it because it was so pretty.'

Esther nodded. She couldn't for the life of her

remember where it was, but she could certainly recall Charlie telling her about it. It sounded lovely, she had thought at the time.

'I can see it!' Charlie shrieked. 'Live. Look.'

Esther looked. Charlie's phone showed a square filled with cafes, bars, and restaurants, outside of which people were eating, drinking, and having a good time. Although it was almost dark, the square was alive with light and colour.

'Who know such things existed?' Charlie demanded. 'There's a whole lot of them. Wow! Venice, Paris, London – all the big cities. Then there are the popular beaches – Acapulco anyone? – and tonnes of other places. Esther, you've got to stop ogling one piddly little bar in Spain and take a look at all these.'

Esther did as she was told. Finding the site on her own phone, she scrolled rapidly down the page, stopping every now and then to click on a location when it caught her eye. This was so much better than Google Street Maps.

'It's the ultimate in people-watching,' she declared, feeling a bit voyeuristic. Then a thought occurred to her. 'Oh, my God, what if a husband was on a business trip or something and he was going to a place that had one of these webcams? His wife could spy on him!' The way I'm spying on Josh, she thought, then pushed it away. It clearly wasn't the same thing at all.

'And maybe she could catch him with another woman,' Charlie cried, joining in with enthusiasm.

'I wish I'd known about this before Josh went on his stag do,' Esther said, suddenly sombre. 'I might have caught him snogging someone else. You can't tell me he's buggered off to Spain just like that without there being a girl involved.'

'From what I saw of the Pink Flamingo, there are loads of girls,' Charlie pointed out. 'He can take his pick, have a different one every night if he wants. Why would he settle for just one?'

Esther's face crumpled. What Charlie said was true. No wonder Josh had left her and his life in England. Over there, with all those girls on holiday and up for a good time with a sexy, handsome barman, he'd be spoilt for choice.

That was the real reason he'd upped and left, she guessed. Because if he'd truly loved her, he'd have asked her to go with him. It had been a pipe dream of theirs to move abroad and begin a new life somewhere warm and sunny where you didn't have to wear boots and a thick coat for 70 per cent of the year. If he'd have asked, she'd have gone with him. But he hadn't asked. He'd simply left, and in amongst her feelings of betrayal and anger, and the anguish and the hurt, was a vague feeling of envy. Josh had had the guts to do what many people had only talked or dreamt about.

She just wished he'd loved her enough to take her with him.

CHAPTER 6

Esther discovered that she'd started a trend. She'd woken the next morning with a terrible headache, as a result of both too much wine and too little sleep from spending half the night obsessively watching the webcam. She hadn't spotted Josh, but she had seen lots of scantily clad girls strutting their stuff and knocking back copious glasses of the one hundred or so varieties of gin that the bar boasted.

The first thing she reached for when she forced her sticky, heavy eyelids open was her phone. She hadn't really expected to see a text from Josh but disappointment washed over her all the same. Automatically, she logged onto the Pink Flamingo's webcam and wasn't surprised to find that the bar was deserted.

However, she did have a message from Sinead.

Thanks for discovering the webcam site, Est, it's fab. See you lunchtime xxx

Charlie must have told Sinead about it. To be fair, it wasn't Esther who had found it, it had been Charlie. The Pink Flamingo's webcam was on its own page and she guessed it would be hard to find it if you weren't actively looking for it, the way she had been.

As Esther dived into the shower in a vain attempt to bring some life back into her lethargic body, she wondered how many more sites with webcams there were in the world.

You couldn't walk down a high street without being filmed, everyone knew that, but before yesterday it would never have occurred to her that she might be filmed when she was sitting in a coffee shop with friends or sharing a meal at her favourite restaurant.

That wasn't totally accurate, she amended, dragging a pair of black trousers and a cream blouse out of her wardrobe; nearly every business had a security camera.

They were part of the fixtures and fittings and no one noticed them anymore (except if you were a criminal and you were planning on burgling the place). What she hadn't realised was that those companies and businesses could broadcast their CCTV to the whole world for anyone to view.

It was a rather disturbing thought, and one she was still musing on when she dashed into work a full twenty minutes late.

'Sorry, sorry!' she cried, rushing over to her desk and dropping into her chair

'Are you OK?' Sally asked, concern on her face. 'After, your, you know…' She leant towards Esther and mouthed, 'Women's problems?'

Eh? 'Uh, oh, yes, better, thanks.'

'You don't look well,' Sally said, and Esther realised that yesterday's bombshell together with a horrid hangover must still be showing on her face.

'I'm OK. I'll soldier on,' she added, womanfully. She'd have to, wouldn't she? She didn't exactly have much choice, although she would have preferred to be in a job where she was rushed off her feet, because she had far too much time to think in this one. Which was why she found herself nipping off to the toilet every few minutes to check on the Pink Flamingo's webcam. She honestly didn't expect to see much action before mid-afternoon, but she couldn't seem to stop herself from looking.

'Are you sure you should be at work?' Sally asked her, after Esther's fourth visit to the little girls' room in an hour.

Esther shrugged. 'I have to be, if I want to get paid.'

It was all right for Sally and the rest of them; they were all employed by the bank. Esther was a temp. If she didn't work, she didn't earn any money. And now that she was on her own in the flat, she'd have to pay all the bills by herself.

Oh, God. That was something else to consider – the rent. It was due at the end of the month and she would bet her right arm that Josh would have cancelled his half of the direct debit. Damn you Josh, she thought, you selfish, inconsiderate pig.

The sting of tears caught her unawares and she blinked hard. There was no way she was going to break down in work, she simply wasn't. To take her mind off her ex-boyfriend, she played several games of solitaire on the bank's computer, then played on Google maps. Where did she fancy exploring today? Of course, it would be Malaga. She'd already had a good look at the inside of the Pink Flamingo and now she wanted to see the place from the outside.

By the time she'd virtually wandered through the streets near the bar, in between actually doing some work in the form of booking a couple of appointments and calculating some commission, it was time for lunch.

As usual, she was meeting Sinead. Whenever Esther had a job in town, she and Sinead would grab a sandwich and a drink in a little cafe down one of the side streets.

Her friend was already sitting at a table when Esther got there, her bag on the seat opposite, saving it for her.

'Charlie told me about Josh,' Sinead said without preamble, once they'd given their orders to the waitress. 'The bastard.'

"Bastard" seemed to be the general consensus amongst her friends.

'I never liked him,' Sinead added. 'You're far too good for him. Talk about punching above his weight.'

That also seemed to be the general opinion, and she was grateful for the way her friends rallied around her and closed ranks.

'Have you seen him yet?' Sinead asked. 'On the webcam, I mean. I can't believe you can watch people online, like that. It's a bit creepy, but terribly addictive.'

Esther picked up the sandwich which had just been placed on the table in front of her and took a bite. She wasn't awfully hungry, but she knew she had to eat. Around a mouthful of spicy chicken, she replied, 'I know, it's scary, isn't it? I wonder if Josh knows about it?'

'If he does, I bet it's never occurred to him that you'd be watching. I had a quick look last night but I didn't see him.'

'I haven't seen him either,' Esther admitted, and she reached for her phone to check yet again. 'Nope, nothing. It looks like no one starts work there until three in the afternoon.'

Sinead didn't appear to be listening. Her eyes were roving around the walls and ceiling of the café and she looked incredibly shifty, as if she was casing the joint.

'What are you doing?' Esther asked.

'Seeing if there are any cameras. There's one over by the till, see?' Sinead jerked her head, her eyes wide, her mouth hardly moving as she added, 'Do you think it's filming us? '

'There wouldn't be any point in it being there if it wasn't,' she pointed out dryly.

'No, silly. I meant do you think it's streaming the images on the internet?'

It was Esther's turn to widen her eyes. 'Ooh! I never thought of that.' Josh knew she always came to this cafe when she had work in town. He could be watching her this very minute, and the thought sent a shiver down her spine. Maybe he still cared about her?

Then common sense kicked in. Of course he didn't care. If he had, he wouldn't have walked out. And he wouldn't be watching her, either. She was letting her imagination run riot. The idea would never occur to him. He was far too selfish to wonder what she was up to or whether she was coping without him.

Sinead grabbed her phone off the table and began thumbing it. After a few minutes she looked up and breathed a sigh of relief. 'It's OK, I can't find anything to suggest we're being filmed.'

'Good, that puts my mind at rest, although when I get back to work I'm going to check there's nothing in my office.'

'You work in a bank, Es. There are cameras everywhere,' Sinead pointed out, which made Esther a little paranoid as she strolled back into work and tried to casually look at the walls and ceilings to check for cameras. It was a good idea to know where they were located, she thought, in case anyone was checking on how many times she nipped off to the loo.

Then she spent the rest of the afternoon trying to resist the urge to do exactly that every five minutes to look at Flamingo Cam, and wondering how she'd fallen so low.

CHAPTER 7

That went well, Kit thought, as he left the offices of Smith, Smythe and Crosby and drove home. From the impression Harvey had given him, he'd been expecting a fresh-faced youth straight out of law school, but Nash Layton was just north of thirty, a smart, intelligent, straight-talking guy with a no-nonsense attitude. He called a spade a spade, and Kit found he liked him, even when the solicitor warned that the case could cost him an arm and a leg and any amount of flesh in between.

'I'm not going to let her take everything,' Kit had declared emphatically, when Nash had run through several possible scenarios.

'It probably won't come to that,' Nash said, 'especially since there aren't any dependent children, but you can never predict exactly who will be awarded what. The court has quite considerable powers of discretion.'

Thank God Nancy and he *didn't* have any children, Kit thought, unable to imagine the heartache a divorce would cause them. Actually, if they *had* had kids, then Kit would have done everything under the sun to keep the family together. He'd fought hard enough to keep the relationship going as it was; until she'd dropped her bombshell about wanting a divorce, that is. And he'd hardly come to terms with the enormity of that, when he'd received the letter from her solicitor. So, now, the gloves were well and truly off, and instead of a straight-forward ending of their marriage, they would have to go to court and let some judge decide whether Kit would end up with nothing.

'Unless you can raise some capital, you will probably have to sell the house,' Nash was saying, 'although I doubt the judge will award your wife as much as 50 per cent. They'll take things into account, such as how long you lived there previous to her moving in, and how much she contributed to the mortgage, the bills and the upkeep, what her future financial prospects are and her ability to work, and then award her a settlement accordingly.'

The thought of selling his beloved cottage made Kit's heart constrict every time the possibility was mentioned. He'd put his heart and soul into that house, especially the garden. Oh, *the garden* – how could he bear to leave it? It had been a labour of love, time, and blistered hands to transform it from an overgrown wasteland filled with nettles and brambles, into the tranquil oasis it was today.

He bet Nancy couldn't care less about him having to sell up. She'd never liked the cottage. She moaned that its original windows had been too draughty, the original fireplace was too dirty, and she'd found the garden too wild and natural for her taste. Actually, she'd never thought much of his choice of career ("glorified gardener" she'd called him once), and she thought the village that he loved so much was a "boring throwback to the 1950s". Never mind that the properties there were sought after and cost a fortune. Never mind that the village was a close-knit community and that crime rates were almost non-existent. Never mind that he'd lived in Middlewick all his life and her scorn for the place cut him deeply.

She'd hated living there, and from the minute she'd moved in she'd nagged at him for them to move. That was one of the reasons the marriage had failed. The other was that he now realised that she'd never really loved him, despite the vows she'd made in church.

And Kit? He'd meant his. Every single word.

Breathing deeply, he got out of the car and inhaled

the scents of the thousands of flowers that grew along the verges of Wildflower Lane and in his own garden. Combined with the sweet smell of freshly mown grass and the earthier aroma of recently turned-over soil from his neighbour's vegetable patch, it was a perfume to soothe the soul. Kit could lose himself for hours in his garden, trimming and weeding, planting and digging, and it never failed to calm and ground him. He could stomp into his garden in the foulest of moods yet emerge from it after a couple of hours wondering what it was that had upset him in the first place.

Hurriedly changing into his work clothes, he hastened out of the kitchen door and into the secluded garden at the rear of the house. It was technically overlooked by his neighbours on either side, but the boundary between his property and the next was blurred by trees and well-established shrubs, which gave it a feeling of privacy. Like the front one, this garden teemed with flowers and insects, and birds darted amongst the branches, chattering excitedly to each other.

Immediately outside the floor-to-ceiling living room doors, was a paved patio, with moss growing between the uneven flagstones, and a rustic table and chairs sitting on it. The whole area was surrounded by a random and eclectic variety of pots. An old coal scuttle contained a vibrant rose bush, each stem tipped with a lipstick pink bloom, and Kit trailed his fingers over the flowers as he passed, feeling the silky softness of the petals and smiling. This particular variety was called Sir John Betjeman, and he'd taken many cuttings from it over the years. In fact, he had a couple in his greenhouse right now, busily sprouting away growing new shoots and roots.

Although there were trees either side of his garden, the rear of it was open, giving him a marvellous view of the fields behind his property. Even with a little white picket fence and the gate set into it marking the actual boundary of his property, it seemed as though everything beyond was an extension of the garden. He loved the open aspect, the way the shrubs and trees framed the view, and the way the landscape stretched for miles into the rolling-hilled distance. Sometimes, sitting out here, he had the feeling that there was no one else in the world but him.

Nancy never saw it that way. The view unsettled her. She had found all that space disconcerting and when he wasn't at home she had complained of feeling isolated and lonely.

How she could feel like that in a village full of people, he had no idea. He only had to stick his nose out of his front door to be greeted by several neighbours and the frequent dog walkers. He knew everyone, and everyone knew him.

Nancy knew no one and hadn't bothered to try to make friends. She used to speed off into town in her little Golf at every opportunity, whether it was to go shopping, to visit friends, to have her hair done, a manicure, a facial – the list of reasons why she needed to visit the city were as varied as they were endless.

He hadn't minded. Whatever made her happy, made him happy.

But she hadn't been happy, had she? She'd been downright miserable.

He hoped she was happier now. He really did. Despite the arguments, the acrimony, and the bitterness, despite her wanting the shirt off his back, despite everything, he hoped she was in a better place emotionally than she'd been when they'd been a couple. He didn't wish her any ill-will, he just wished she'd stop being so greedy.

Thinking about his estranged wife was making him uneasy, so to distract himself he wandered to the end of the garden, opened the little gate and stepped into the world of fields, hedgerows and woodland. But his favourite part was the area immediately outside the garden. Not too many months ago the field had contained several quite valuable horses. Breeding mares, he'd been told, and all of them in foal. But when the time drew nearer for them to give birth, the farmer who owned them had moved them to fields closer to his house, and so far they'd yet to return. Which meant that the grass had grown incredibly long, and when left to its own devices the field had turned into a wildflower meadow, probably having been seeded by the plants in his own garden.

The only eyesore (and it wasn't even that, if he was honest) was a large shelter erected for the mares, but considering he couldn't really see it from his garden it didn't bother him.

Letting nature soothe his ragged emotions, he stayed in the meadow until the light began to fade from the sky, hoping and praying that he wouldn't be forced to give up his lovely home.

CHAPTER 8

Esther's old laptop was a little dusty (she'd found it under the bed – *their* bed, the one she had shared with Josh) and was rather slow, but it did the trick. She usually did everything on her phone, which was why she'd shoved the computer under there in the first place because it was more or less obsolete. On her short commute home she'd remembered it and hoped she'd found a solution to her aching eyes – a bigger screen.

It took a while to fire up, so she let it download six million and one updates while she warmed up a frozen meal and took the half a bottle of wine which was all that was left after last night's excesses, out of the fridge and poured herself a glass. By the time the lasagne was piping hot the laptop had done its thing and was raring to go. Actually, trundling to go would be a better description, she thought, as she waited for it to consider her request to log on as she spooned her meal out of the carton and onto a plate. Then she settled down at the table in the living room and found the site.

Nothing was happening. It was showing an empty bar and she wondered if the laptop was still buffering. Darn it, she'd been looking forward to not having to try to zoom in on her phone every time she thought she'd caught a glimpse of Josh, but it looked as though the ancient laptop was struggling to cope.

Defeated, she fetched her mobile.

Nothing was happening on that, either.

In desperation she went back to the laptop, and it was then she spotted a long list of comments, most of them posted in the last hour or so, and all of them complaining that the site was down.

Esther blew out her cheeks in frustration. Doubting there'd be any other sites that would show the interior of the Pink Flamingo, she looked anyway, but didn't find anything. Getting cross, she started flicking around other webcams, like the ones showing St Mark's Square in Venice and the beach in Barcelona. Some cities had several webcams which could be accessed, others had none, and the coverage was a bit hit and miss. She found one showing the promenade in Los Cristianos in Tenerife which also had sound and she spent far too long listening to a bar just out of shot which was hosting some of the most dreadful karaoke that she'd heard in a long time. And in between songs she could even hear the sounds of cutlery on plates and people's muffled voices. Despite turning the volume on the speakers up and straining to hear what they were saying, she couldn't quite make the words out. But it wasn't for want of trying.

This was the ultimate in people-watching, she thought, and she trawled around, clicking on pages and seeing where they would lead, sipping her wine, and every now and again checking to see if Flamingo Cam was working again.

Abruptly, she straightened up as a new and considerably different kind of image appeared on her screen. What was *that*? It looked like someone's living room. She could see into the kitchen too. And a bit of the bedroom. How weird. Was it a film set of some kind? It didn't look like it, but then again what did she know about film sets and TV and stuff?

Esther refilled her glass and carried on watching. Nothing much was happening. Nothing at all actually, a bit like Flamingo Cam she thought, as she flicked back to the bar. "Nothing much happening" seemed to be the story of her life at the moment.

Ooh, hang on! Flamingo Cam went black, flickered a little, then came back on in all its live, technicolour glory.

And there he was. Her Josh. Standing behind the bar as if he'd been there for months and not just for a few days, dressed up to the nines in a black button-down shirt with the sleeves rolled up to show off his forearms, and a tan he hadn't had the last time she'd seen him. Her boyfriend looked good. He also looked happier than she'd seen him for months. Her boyfriend—

Actually, he wasn't her boyfriend anymore, was he? He wasn't *her* Josh.

Her heart ached so much at the sight of him that she thought it might burst. He was laughing, his head thrown back, teeth gleaming whiter than she had ever seen them (maybe he'd had them whitened at the same time he'd had the spray tan), and she wished he was laughing for her or with her, and not for the benefit of those floozies draped across the bar, with their long tanned legs, big boobs, and flouncy hair.

It wasn't fair.

If he'd had said he was unhappy and said he wanted a change, she'd have done her best to make it happen. If he'd come back from Malaga and told her that this Andy-guy had offered him a job and he wanted to take him up on it and move out to Spain for a few months to see how he liked it, she would have gone with him. Of course she would have. She might have argued about it for a bit because they hadn't been in their little flat for a year yet, but she would have gone. After all, she didn't have a job she needed to jack in and she was pretty certain she would have been able to find work out there.

But he hadn't given her the option, had he? He'd just buggered off without even kissing her goodbye.

'I hate you,' she said, watching as he laughed and joked with anyone who came within earshot. He was pouring drinks as if he'd been doing it all his life, with confidence and panache. And she hated him for it.

She also hated that he was having so much fun without her. She hated that he was clearly loving this new life of his. She hated that he didn't appear to be missing her at all. But most of all she hated that she still loved him after what he'd done to her.

And, to top it all off, she hated herself for feeling that way.

CHAPTER 9

Esther kicked off her shoes and slung her bag in the general direction of the sofa before padding out to the kitchen in her stocking feet, a stack of envelopes in her hand.

House insurance, car tax reminder (Josh's, not hers), letter from the bank... Meh. Nothing interesting. The one from the bank was probably advising her that she was overdrawn.

'Tell me something I don't know,' she muttered, throwing them on the worktop. She'd deal with them later. Probably sometime in the next century.

As usual, she dug a meal out of the freezer and popped it in the microwave. She used to stock those in case of emergencies or if Josh was going out and she couldn't be bothered to cook for herself but since he'd left, ready-meals were becoming a staple part of her diet. She realised that the situation needed to change but right now the thought of going to all that effort to produce a meal just for one was simply exhausting.

While she waited for it to heat up, she turned the laptop on and began to scroll. This was also becoming a bit of a habit, she realised, and one she should break, even though she also realised that she didn't want to. It gave her some weird tortured comfort to watch him every evening, as if she was still a part of his life.

Not much was happening on Flamingo Cam this evening, except for a bit of mopping and wiping over of tables by the cleaning staff, but in the cold light of day the whole place looked as if it could benefit from a good scrub. It was marvellous what could be achieved with some disco balls and twinkly lights, she thought, clicking off the site and deciding to have a look at what was going on in the rest of the world.

The square in front of the cathedral in Milan was busy, there were elephants at a waterhole in Kenya, and the sky over Dubai was an ominous orange from an encroaching dust storm. She watched the elephants for a bit, making little cooing noises when she saw a baby throwing its trunk around, and wished she could share the moment with Josh. And although she quite enjoyed viewing all these far-off places and it gave her something to do to occupy her time, it wasn't the same without someone to share the experience with.

She scrolled on, travelling Europe one webcam at a time until finally her thoughts turned back to the Pink Flamingo and Josh. Wait a minute though, wasn't that the other site, the strange one showing what seemed to be someone's living room? She clicked on it, curiously, wondering what it actually was. She hadn't taken a great deal of notice last time, except for thinking that it was a bit weird and she wouldn't like it if there was a camera pointing directly into her living room, but this time she pushed her plate to one side and leant forward for a closer look.

The camera seemed to be located at the rear of a house, with a view of most of a living room and part of a kitchen on the ground floor, and a bedroom and a window with frosted glass which she assumed was a bathroom, on the top floor. The angle of the camera didn't allow her to see into the bedroom (which was probably a good thing), but the downstairs rooms were quite clear indeed.

She guesstimated that the camera was about fifty or so feet away from the little house, although she could be wrong because she wasn't particularly good with distances. And it must be a few feet off the ground, as the camera was looking down slightly, rather than straight in. Which was a shame, Esther thought, because she would have liked to have had a better view of the whole of the living room, not just a part of it.

The house looked nice. Built of butter-coloured stone with wooden windows and ivy growing up the side, the living room had a pair of French doors leading out onto a bit of a patio. But it wasn't the outside that interested her – it was the inside.

She could make out a part of a sofa and a squashy chair covered in light grey fabric, a pale grey rug on a polished wooden floor, a real fireplace, and a picture hanging above it. She thought she could see the edge of a TV peeking out from behind one of the curtains framing the French doors, but she wasn't certain. The kitchen, which she could see far less of, sported white units, and a man staring out of the window.

Esther almost ducked out of sight until she realised that even though he might be staring directly into the camera, there was no way on earth he could see her.

Or even know that anyone was watching him.

Actually, she didn't think he was really looking at the camera, just in its general direction, and every so often he'd glance down and his arm would move and she realised he must be doing the washing up. Her guess proved to be correct when she saw him reach for a cloth and dry his hands.

He was quite good-looking she noticed, with broad

shoulders, the sort of jaw that magazines called chiselled, and short dark brown hair with the odd lock or two flopping over his forehead.

He was good-looking *from this distance*, she amended. Close up he might not be so attractive. She thought he might have nice-shaped lips too, but it wasn't easy to tell, and she desperately wished she was close enough to see his eyes. She had a feeling they might be hazel, or maybe even green...

He turned away from the window and walked out of shot, and with the spell broken Esther shook herself. What was she doing ogling another guy when her own was God-knows how many miles away and—

Ogling other girls, she saw when she clicked onto Flamingo Cam.

Josh, this time in a skin-tight T-shirt to show off his chest and abs, was leaning across the bar and peering down some tart's cleavage. Not that he had far to peer, because the girl practically had all her assets on show and was halfway to shoving them in Josh's face. Esther narrowed her eyes. She knew exactly what *she* wanted to shove in Josh's face and it wasn't a pair of boobs. She would start with her fist and see where she went from there.

Who was she kidding? If he was here right now the only thing she would do would be to wrap her arms around him and tell him how much she loved him and missed him, and no doubt she'd humiliate herself by begging him to come back.

The flat felt terribly empty without him; she'd never been so lonely. What was she supposed to do with her life now? They'd had so many plans, so many ideas about their future together and he'd gone and thrown it all away. And he'd thrown her away along with them.

Tears, hot and stinging, filled her eyes and spilt over to trickle down her cheeks.

She should be done crying over that man but she couldn't help it, and it was a long time before she brought herself back under control. When she finally did, she made a vow – she'd give herself a little more time to grieve and then she intended to sort her life out. If Josh could do it, then so could she.

CHAPTER 10

Kit was so tired he didn't know what to do with himself. Keeping busy was the best remedy for too much thinking, his dad always said, so that's exactly what he'd been doing. Keeping busy was a bit of an understatement, though – he'd been working himself to the bone and he couldn't seem to stop. Not even now, when he might fall asleep standing up while trying to wash the dishes. In fact, he could feel his eyes closing and he jerked awake, anxious to avoid dropping a plate.

At least he'd made something to eat, because lately he'd been living off sandwiches and the occasional meal at the Willow and Wicket. The pub was nice enough and he used to go there fairly often, but the problem with living in a small community was exactly the same as the advantage of living in one – everyone knew everyone else's business, and everyone felt free to offer sympathy and advice in copious and unasked for amounts. Which tended to put him off going there, when all he wanted was a hot meal, a pint and to be left alone. The last time he'd visited the pub, he'd been the recipient of so many pitying looks and pats on the shoulder that he'd wondered whether someone had died and nobody'd had the heart to tell him.

This evening Dean had sent him home with a flea in his ear. He'd only been trying to help by working in the office (anything to keep busy and the paperwork desperately needed doing) but had kept interrupting him to ask about this, that and the other. His brother had been trying to concentrate on working on a design for an Elizabethan garden for a stately home refurbishment, and hadn't appreciated having his concentration repeatedly broken.

Which was why he was banished to his cottage, too tired to face doing any manual work in his own garden (not that anything really needed doing because he'd done it all), but too restless to sit still. So he'd cooked a meal and had eaten it while trying to read a trade magazine and keep his eyes open at the same time.

The plate he was attempting to wash slipped back into the soapy water with a splash, and he jumped a little. He'd been staring unseeing into the garden, his jumbled thoughts tumbling repeatedly through his head. Thoughts such as where he was going to live if he was forced to sell, and whether he'd be given enough time to find the right sort of buyer, the type of person who'd love the garden just the way it was, and not dig it up and put in a ruddy great big lawn instead. Or, and he shuddered at the idea, deck it all and stick a hideous trampoline or a hot tub slap bang in the middle.

No, he wanted someone who would appreciate the hard work and effort that had gone into making this garden so special. Someone who'd love it as much as he did. But he had an awful feeling that beggars couldn't be choosers and that he'd be forced to take the highest offer.

The sting of tears took him by surprise and he blinked them away furiously. He wouldn't cry. *He wouldn't*, he vowed.

But he did, and when the tears fell fast and hot, he left the washing up, reached for a towel and hastily dried his hands, before stumbling up the stairs to seek the sweet oblivion that sleep would bring. For a few hours, at least.

CHAPTER 11

Esther wasn't really in the mood for a night out, especially when the other six people sitting at the table were all coupled up and one of her friends had invited a stray guy along. Esther wasn't sure whether it was to even up the numbers (spare wheel?) or to try to set her up with a date.

She was acutely conscious that it should have been Josh sitting next to her and not some stranger, although the guy seemed nice enough. But he wasn't Josh, and every other time she'd gone out with Charlie, Sinead, Abbie and their respective partners, she'd been one half of a couple. Being single when all your friends were loved up, sucked. The whole evening had been awkward. What was she supposed to say to this man? And he clearly felt as awkward as she did.

'So,' he began, when everyone else except him and

her seemed deep in conversation. 'You're Esther.'

She nodded. 'And you're Dean.'

He nodded back.

Around them, their friends were busy laughing and chatting, catching up on news and gossip. Esther could join in, but she felt sorry for this outsider. At least she knew the others really well. This poor guy appeared to only know Steve, Abbie's boyfriend, so she felt a kind of obligation to make him feel welcome, even as part of her vowed to have a few words with the others later. Did they honestly think she was ready to date again? Josh had only been gone a couple of weeks, and although they might have thought she would feel awkward being the only singleton in the group, she'd have coped with it rather than have to deal with such an embarrassing situation.

'Where do you work?' Dean asked.

'I'm temping in a bank in Worcester,' she said. 'What about you?'

'A small firm in Middlewick.'

'Doing what?' she wanted to know. Actually, she wasn't particularly interested. She couldn't care less about what he did, but she felt obliged to keep the conversation going. Whose idea was it to ask this guy along, anyway? When she found out, she'd give them a piece of her mind.

'I'm a landscape gardener,' he said.

‘Oh.’ That was it then, Esther had nothing more to say. She didn’t have the faintest idea about gardening. The nearest she ever came to a plant was to buy the occasional bunch of flowers to brighten up the living room or take a stroll around the park now and again.

She decided to change tack. ‘Seen any good bands recently?’ Not that she had, but everyone liked music, right?

‘I prefer classical music,’ he said. ‘I don’t do the modern stuff much.’

Great. What she knew about classical music could be written on the back of a postage stamp and still leave plenty of room to spare. She sent a glare around the table. The others were either engrossed in their conversations or were pretending to be, so she’d not get any help from them.

‘I do like wine, though,’ Dean said, pushing his chair back and getting to his feet. ‘Another round?’

Her friends heard that all right, Esther noticed sourly, as they hastily finished their drinks and held out their glasses. A chorus of, ‘cheers, mate,’ and, ‘mine’s a glass of red, please,’ followed.

She watched him until he’d walked far enough away, then she turned to Steve and hissed, ‘Was this your idea?’

Steve grimaced. ‘Er… not really.’ He shot his girlfriend a desperate look.

'It was yours then, was it?' she asked Abbie.

'I thought you might feel a bit left out,' Abbie replied, biting her lip. She glanced around at the rest for support and they all nodded.

'Thanks for nothing,' Esther muttered.

'He's a great guy, once you get to know him,' Steve said.

'I've got no intention of getting to know him,' Esther stated. 'Not tonight, not ever.'

'Look, I know it's a bit soon after Josh, but you've got to get back on the horse sometime,' Charlie said.

'No, I don't. I'm off men for the time being. I'm going to concentrate on my career.'

Esther saw the surreptitious glances that her friends gave each other, and she immediately felt disconsolate. They clearly thought she didn't have a career, and she had a horrid feeling they were right. She was twenty-seven and all she'd done since leaving school was work at a succession of temping jobs. It wasn't much to show for ten years of employment, but, damn it, she was good at her job – *jobs*. She had gained a wealth of experience working in all kinds of admin roles; surely she could put some of it to good use?

Dean came back with several drinks balanced precariously on a tray and handed them out. Esther took her gin and tonic absently. Her mind was still on her future – or lack of it.

Should she do something drastic, like go to university? A degree would give her something to add to her CV, but the question was, what did she want to study? She had absolutely no idea what she wanted to do or what she might be good at. Anyway, having a degree didn't guarantee you a job these days. She'd lost count of the number of people who'd signed up with the same agency that she was with, who had a degree but couldn't get a job. Besides, she couldn't afford to return to education – she had rent and bills to pay, which was going to be considerably harder now that Josh wasn't there to share the financial burden.

Esther assumed that her declaration of wanting to concentrate on her career had been swept under the carpet, but when Charlie had taken a sip of her drink she leant forward and said, 'What are you thinking of doing? Have you got anything in mind?'

In all honesty, Esther hadn't. But she realised that with marriage and babies currently off the table, she had to do something with her life. Before she knew it she'd be thirty and with little to show for being on the planet for three whole decades. Talk about being stuck in a rut…

She shrugged. 'I dunno, but I'm sick to death of temping.'

She used to love working in different places, never staying with one assignment for long (the longest stint had been six months in an estate agent when the receptionist had fallen unexpectedly pregnant), learning new skills, and meeting new people. She'd always assumed she'd get bored working for the same company year in year out, but in all honesty, she was bored out of her mind now. She preferred to be busy; she always had, and it made the day go quicker. She hated clock-watching. And she realised she was also beginning to dislike the constant change and the fact that she didn't have a hope in hell of promotion, although with her experience she was frequently offered the more responsible and prestigious assignments. The problem was they were few and far between.

Josh's leaving had made her realise that professionally she was stuck in a rut. It hadn't mattered when he was there to come home to every evening, but with him gone she felt as though the spark had faded from every area of her life.

Charlie was persistent. 'What would you say you're good at?'

'Um... organising?' She tapped her fingers against her cheek, thinking.

'That's a start. What else?'

'Customer relations, reception work, data input.'

Esther was on a roll. 'Answering phones, using spreadsheets, um... photocopying? Typing letters.' Now she was starting to scrape the bottom of the barrel.

'It sounds like you'd make a good PA,' Dean interjected.

Esther blinked. She hadn't realised he'd been listening, having assumed he was joining in with the lively conversation which was taking place between the three men regarding last night's footie scores. If Josh had been here, he'd have been in the thick of it and arguing goals and penalties until his ears grew pink

'I would, wouldn't I?' she mused. It wouldn't be too far removed from anything she'd done in the past. In fact, she'd done *exactly* that sort of thing in the past, as she'd had a couple of stints at PA work and had quite enjoyed it. But working so closely with one person meant that you really had to get on with your boss, and those type of jobs tended to be quite hotly contested. She knew that they paid well too, if you were lucky enough to get in with one of the bigger companies.

'I'll have a look online when I get home,' she said, imagining herself working for the CEO of an international company and travelling all over the world with him or her. She'd be like Andy in *The Devil*

Wears Prada, but more clued-in and switched-on, and with better dress-sense – until that fella, what was his name, got involved and gave Andy half a tonne of freebies and taught her how to wear them. She could do with a few designer pieces herself, Esther mused. Good quality clothes that didn't date. Not that she could afford any – Primark was about her limit.

'There's a vacancy at my place,' Dean said, bringing her back to earth.

'Eh?'

'I said, there's a vacancy for a personal assistant at LandScape Ltd,' Dean repeated.

'Oh, right.' That wasn't the kind of thing she'd been imagining, but OK, she'd give it a go. No doubt she'd have to do a stint or two in a couple of smaller companies first, before she could apply to one of the bigger ones and land the job of her (very recent) dreams.

'Here.' He took his wallet out of his pocket and pulled out a business card, handing it to her. She studied it, running her fingers across its creamy, embossed surface.

Dean Reynolds, Landscape Gardener it said, along with a landline number, an email address and details of their website.

'Thanks. Shall I ring for an application form or send my CV?' she asked

'Your CV will do,' he said. 'Email it directly to me. Right, must be off, I've got an early start tomorrow.' He finished his pint in one long swallow. 'Make sure you send me your CV,' he added, as he got to his feet.

'I will,' she promised. And she would, too. She'd also mention his name in her covering letter, because sometimes when it came to jobs, it wasn't so much what you know, as who you know, and Esther wasn't ashamed to plug his name if it got her an interview.

It was only as she was getting ready for bed later that evening, she realised that she hadn't checked Flamingo Cam once.

CHAPTER 12

Josh wasn't in the bar this afternoon. No one was. It was too early for anyone except the cleaners, but even they hadn't shown up yet. There was someone in the living room of the little cottage, though. She hadn't meant to look, but she'd been scrolling around, clicking on various links, when the cottage had popped up on her screen and she hadn't been able to resist, especially when she realised the man was at home.

He was prowling around his living room, a phone held to his ear, and from his expression, Esther guessed he wasn't enjoying the conversation much. He kept waving his free arm around, and every now and again he shook his head. Once or twice he stopped pacing and looked at the phone with what she could only assume was an expression of disbelief.

She was fascinated and a little appalled at the same

time, wondering how he'd react if he knew he was being watched in his own home by a total stranger. She wouldn't be at all happy if she was in his shoes, and she knew she should close the page down, but she simply couldn't stop watching.

At least he wasn't doing anything repulsive, like clipping his nose hairs or wandering around in the nude. Actually, seeing him naked mightn't be at all horrible, she amended. He looked pretty darned good with his clothes on, and she could only imagine how much better he might look with them off.

'Don't be such a pervert,' she muttered under her breath, hoping she wasn't turning into the sort of person who'd peer through other people's windows, or hide a camera in a hotel room. The line between that kind of thing and what she was doing was very slim indeed. If she knew where he lived, she'd pay him a visit and tell him what was going on, because it simply wasn't right…

Or would she? She had a sudden vision of knocking on his door and trying to explain that she'd been ogling him on her laptop, and she had a feeling the conversation wouldn't go all that well. If she was him, she'd want to know, but she was pretty sure she'd shoot the messenger too. Either that, or she'd call the police. And she wasn't totally sure that what she was doing was strictly legal, even though she wasn't the person who had put the camera up in the first place or had trained it on his house.

Then she wondered who had and what they'd hoped to gain from it. Maybe Cottage Cam had been put there by the police or the secret service because he was a drug dealer or a spy, and someone had pressed the wrong button, allowing the footage to be streamed publicly.

The back of her neck tingled with excitement at the possibilities. She might even be called as a witness if something were to happen.

She stared at the screen again, expecting... something. She wasn't sure what exactly, but she was fully prepared for it. But all Cottage Cam Man did was to stuff his phone into his back pocket, march into the kitchen and grab a can out of the fridge. Then he stomped back into the living room and sat down. At least, that's what she assumed he did, when the majority of him disappeared from view to be replaced by a pair of trainer-clad feet on a coffee table.

Esther tutted under her breath. Either he lived alone or his wife/girlfriend was out, because she didn't know any female on the planet who'd let their man plonk their dirty, great feet on a piece of furniture that was designed to hold a plate of custard creams. Josh would never have dreamt of doing anything so laddish.

Hang on a minute; or *would he*? Because he'd done the ultimate in laddish and had buggered off to Spain to work in a wine bar, so God knows what he used to get up to when she wasn't around. With that thought circling in her head, she checked Flamingo Cam again. Still nothing to see.

She was actually getting quite fed up with having to stay awake most of the night to try to catch a glimpse of her beloved. And then when she did see him he was usually staring down a girl's cleavage while shaking a cocktail holder and waggling his hips at the same time. Who said men couldn't multi-task!

She jumped when her phone rang. It was Charlie.

'I wanted to check how you were doing after last night,' her friend said.

'Ok, I guess. I mean, I still haven't forgiven you guys for setting me up on a blind date, but at least I got to hear about a possible job.'

'Have you applied for it?' Charlie wanted to know.

'I sent off my CV as soon as I got up this morning,' Esther confirmed.

'What are you doing tonight?'

Watching other people getting on with their lives while I sit at home and let mine slip through my fingers, Esther nearly said, but didn't. 'Nothing much.'

'Do you fancy popping over? I've got some wine chilling in the fridge and a family-size packet of Maltesers in the cupboard.'

That was an offer Esther couldn't refuse. It was far better than sitting on her own in her dismal little flat on a Friday night, and it was about time the pair of them had a decent catch-up.

Charlie opened one of the bottles as soon as Esther dropped wearily down onto the sofa, and handed her a glass. She took it with a sigh and downed half the contents in one go.

'Slow down, girlie, you'll be drunk before you know it if you carry on at this rate,' Charlie said.

'You'd better drink your share then,' she retorted, 'before I finish the lot off. Although getting blotto seems like a really good idea. Anything that would make me forget how sad and awful my life is right now, would be welcome.'

'Have you been on that webcam site again? It's not healthy, you know. Seeing your ex splashing his life all over Facebook or Instagram would be bad enough, but watching him live isn't going to help you get over him, not to mention that it's a bit stalkerish.'

Esther had to agree that it was, although she didn't admit that to her friend. And neither did she admit to spending rather a long time this afternoon staring at a complete stranger in his own home, because that really *was* bordering on perverse. But when the other option was watching some programme about antiques on the telly or a film she'd seen a hundred times before, she knew which she preferred.

'What you need is a holiday; something to look forward to.' Charlie refilled Esther's empty glass and topped up her own.

Once again, Esther drank half of hers immediately.

With a sigh, Charlie followed suit, and Esther grinned at the show of camaraderie. It was no fun getting half-cut on your own, although she'd have to slow down a bit because she had work in the morning. They both did.

'I can't afford a holiday,' she said. 'Don't forget, I have to pay for everything myself now.'

'There's nothing stopping you from having a look. You can find lots of bargains by booking at the last minute. I wish I could go somewhere nice and hot and lie on a sunbed for a couple of weeks. Heck, even one week would do. I'm not greedy.'

'Where would you go? Spain?'

'Maybe. Or Greece. As long as I can wear a bikini without getting frostbite, I'd be happy.'

'Why don't you book something?'

Charlie huffed. 'Jay isn't keen. He keeps saying we need to save hard if we want a bigger house.'

Esther glanced around her friend's small but

perfectly formed living room. Charlie and Jay's house was tiny, but at least it was theirs. 'I've always liked your house. It's cosy.'

'I think the word you're looking for is small.' Charlie grinned. 'I'm not as bothered about moving as Jay is. The larger the house, the more cleaning that needs to be done, and considering I do the lion's share of the housework I'm not too excited about the prospect of having to do more of it.'

'Josh never bothered much either. He always left it all to me. I wonder who's washing his boxers for him now, and ironing those ridiculous shirts he's started wearing,' she said glumly, and to her dismay her eyes began to prickle.

Not again, she thought – she was fed up of feeling so sad all the time. She'd cried bucket loads over him already and, as her friends kept telling her, he wasn't worth it. Her head knew that, but it seemed her heart hadn't received the memo. She was still quite raw, and the slightest thing could set her off.

'Oh, sweetie, he's so not worth it,' Charlie said, scooting closer and pulling her in for a hug.

Esther smiled through her teary sniffles. 'I know. You keep telling me.'

'That's because it's true. You can do so much better than him. You'll find someone else, someone who deserves you, you'll see. Now, shall we have a look at all those lovely holidays we can't afford? You never know, you might see one of those bargains I was talking about. A week away will do you good and help you take your mind off that rat.'

Esther seriously doubted it, but for the next couple of hours she and Charlie trawled various holiday sites, interspersed with looking at webcams in a variety of wonderful and exotic locations and dreaming of the places they would like to visit if they had unlimited funds.

After two bottles of wine, a couple of gins, and the remnants of bottle of Baileys Irish Cream left over from Christmas (didn't this particular drink have a use-by date, Esther mused drunkenly, hoping she wouldn't get food poisoning), she was rather the worse for wear and could hardly see straight.

The evening culminated in her sobbing her heart out – yet again – and announcing she'd never, ever get over Josh. Not in a million years. 'I'm going to stay single forever and have six cats,' she declared. 'Cats are loyal.'

'Nah, you're thinking of dogs,' Charlie hiccupped, slumping back into the sofa, the liquid in her glass slopping over the rim. 'Oops. I'd better clean that up before Jay notices.' She attempted to extricate herself from the cushions but failed miserably, so gave up.

Esther, for some reason, found her friend's antics

hilarious and giggled loudly in between bursts of crying. 'Malaga,' she announced. 'I'm going to Malaga. I'm going to give Josh a piece of my mind and show him what he's missing. And you're coming with me.'

'I don't wanna. I wanna go to Mexico.'

'Malaga's like Mexico,' Esther stated firmly. 'They speak Spanish.'

'Do they? I thought they spoke Mexican.'

Esther took another gulp of Bailey's and pulled a face. 'Spanish,' she replied firmly. 'And it's cheaper. See?' She angled her phone so Charlie could view it.

Charlie squinted. 'Is that each?'

'For two. I told you, I can't go on my own. I'm gonna book it.'

'For real?'

'Yeah.'

'You're not. You can't.'

'I can.' Esther retrieved her purse from her bag after much fumbling and brandished her bank card. 'I've got enough in my account. Just.'

'Finish your drink first. I need to think about it.'

Esther finished her drink. Then had another. She was feeling pretty good, considering the state she'd been in earlier. Maybe Charlie was right and a holiday would do her good. Just thinking about it was making her feel better.

CHAPTER 13

Kit took the phone away from his ear and stared at it incredulously. Nancy must be out of her mind! What on earth was she doing, calling him to tell him she thought she deserved half of his share of the business? For one thing, their respective solicitors were already handling all this. And for another, what right did she have to demand any part of the company that he and Dean had worked so hard to build? She'd contributed nothing to it. *Nothing.*

He put the phone back to his ear. She was still ranting. Was she drunk or something? Did she think that by phoning him directly that she was going to make him roll over and give her everything she wanted? He might have done that in the past, but not anymore.

'Look, Nancy, I don't know how many ways I can say it – I am not letting you have half of my business.'

He was acutely aware that he'd said this through gritted teeth, but darn it, every part of him was tense. She had that effect on him. He couldn't remember the last time they'd spoken civilly to each other, much less the last time there'd been any love in their words.

How had it come to this? He'd never imagined he'd be getting divorced. No one went into marriage with the idea that it mightn't last forever, did they? He certainly hadn't. On his part, he'd pictured the pair of them growing old together, with grandkids on their knees. On hers, he was beginning to wonder if all he'd ever been to her was a meal-ticket, and he had the horrible feeling that he'd been used.

Without saying anything more, because there was nothing more he *could* say to his estranged wife, he ended the call and stuffed the phone angrily into his back pocket. He could really do with a beer, he thought, as he stomped into the kitchen and yanked the fridge door open. Instead, he grabbed a can of cola, and marched back into the living room, throwing himself into a chair. He was meeting Angie soon and there was no way he'd risk driving after drinking alcohol – not even a single beer – so he'd have to make do with a sugar-rush instead.

Angie was another victim of a disastrous marriage, but they hadn't compared notes. She knew he was getting a divorce because he'd told her when they'd met for a quick lunch the other day, but he hadn't shared any of the nastier details with her and he didn't intend to. Angie was in town for such a short time and he wanted to simply enjoy her company and not sully it with talk of ex-spouses.

He'd often thought Kyle wasn't right for her, but when one of your oldest friends falls in love what can you do except support them? Besides, she'd been living in California (she still did) and he'd only met the guy twice, and one of those times was at Angie's wedding. He could hardly tell her she looked beautiful in one breath and express his reservations regarding her new husband in another. He had told her eventually, after the tears and heartache had eased, that he'd never liked Kyle anyway, but it had all been done remotely over the phone or by WhatsApp. He often wished he could have been there more for her, but with about five-thousand miles between them all he could do was send his love and flowers, and hope that one day she'd find happiness again.

He wasn't holding out much hope for his own chances, though. At the moment, he'd just be content to have everything settled between him and Nancy without losing the shirt off his back.

Giving himself a mental shake, he tried out a smile for size and went off to meet his friend.

CHAPTER 14

'I've gotta go home,' Esther said, a considerable while later. Her head felt as though it belonged to someone else and she couldn't keep a thought in it to save her life. She glanced at Charlie, draped upside down in one of the armchairs, her head hanging over the edge of the seat, her legs over the back. Her eyes were closed, her mouth was open, and she was dead to the world.

'Bye, Char,' she said, planting a sloppy kiss on her friend's forehead.

'Gerroff.' Charlie mumbled, flinging an uncoordinated arm in the air and batting her away.

'I'm going,' she told her.

'Mmph.'

'Bye.'

There was no response at all this time, so she grabbed her bag, almost falling over as she reached down for it, then made her way unsteadily towards the door, one hand on the wall for balance.

A taxi, that's what she needed she decided as she pulled the door shut behind her. She'd better order one. Except she couldn't see the screen on her phone properly. There must be something wrong with her eyes, because it was all a bit fuzzy. Perhaps she needed glasses?

'Must go to Specsavers,' she mumbled, then hiccupped. 'Pardon me.' Had anyone heard her? She peered down the street, but it was deserted. And dark. 'That's because it's night time,' she told herself aloud, then clapped a hand to her mouth. Bloody hell, not only was she single, lonely, sad, and drunk, she was now talking to herself.

She really had better go home.

A taxi, that's what she needed, she thought again, and remembered that she'd been about to phone for one. She squinted at her mobile. Ah, good, she could just make out the words *'Pay Now'* on a bright blue button.

These apps are flipping brilliant, she thought. 'Appy Cabs – geddit? He, he, he, she chuckled to herself; every time she used their app she smiled, and tonight was no exception. She'd be very 'appy' to see them indeed, because there was no way she was walking home. She could hardly stand upright for a start.

The *'Pay Now'* button was still on her screen.

She needed to press it.

She pressed it.

'Do you want to pay with this card?' her screen asked her.

She pressed *'Yes'*.

There, done. Now all she had to do was wait. It was a bit of an extravagance but catching a bus at this time of night wasn't an option she wanted to take. It would be full of drunken youngsters and strange men.

Had the app given her a time? It usually did. She checked her phone.

Darn it, the thing was dead. She'd spent so long on all those webcam sites that she'd drained the battery. Bugger. Now she had no idea how long she'd have to wait. It might have been a better idea to have ordered her taxi from *inside* Charlie's house and not *outside*, she thought. Not only did she feel a right idiot loitering around on the street, and she also felt rather vulnerable. An excess of alcohol, a late night and a too-quiet street, wasn't a good combination.

Ah, was that her cab?

Headlights approached, slowed a little, then swept past. Disappointed, she saw that the vehicle was a small, dark van.

Not her taxi, then.

She glanced over her shoulder and noticed that the van had come to a stop further up the street. No one got out, but the engine stayed on. It merely sat there, idling menacingly, its rear lights shining a threatening red.

She carried on watching and it continued to sit there, unmoving.

Oh God, you heard of things like this happening. Was something awful about to happen to her?

She retrieved her keys from her bag, clutching them in one hand, poised to jab them in her would-be assailant's eye, and turned towards Charlie's front door with her fist raised, ready to hammer on it at the slightest hint that the van was coming for her.

More headlights, and this time they flashed at her.

Thank God. Her taxi had arrived.

Esther darted into the road, waving at the car, and as soon as it drew to a halt she yanked the rear door open and slithered inside.

'Go!' she demanded.

The taxi didn't move, but the driver asked, 'Are you OK?'

'No, there's a van, I think it's after me.'

'The van in front?'

Esther leant forward to peer through the windscreen. The van that had pulled over was now in front of them, travelling slowly up the road. 'Yes, that's it. Can you lose it?'

'It's not following us,' the driver told her. 'If anything, *we're* following *it*.'

'Then don't. I don't want to follow it. I want to go home.'

'Where is that?'

Crickey, some of these drivers were useless. Or maybe the taxi firm hadn't sent her details through. She gave him her address and sank back in the seat, shuffling down a bit as the taxi turned right. The van continued to travel along the road they'd just been on, and her eyes remained on the van until it was out of sight before she breathed a sigh of relief.

'Don't worry, I'll make sure you get home safely,' the driver told her.

Good. That *was* kind of his job, but she was grateful all the same. She liked this particular cab company, not just because of the app (so easy to use – too easy?) but also because most of the drivers waited until you'd opened your door and stepped inside before they drove off. Not during the day obviously, but at night, when single women were more vulnerable and...

Single. That's what she was. All alone. There was no one waiting in the flat for her. No one to turn the lamp on. No one to worry if she didn't come home.

A sob slipped out of her.

'Are you all right?' the driver asked. 'Do you want me to call the police? I didn't think to make a note of the registration number.'

'My boyfriend left me.' She sniffed. 'For a Pink Flamingo.'

'Excuse me?'

'Malaga.'

'Okaaay…' There was a pause. 'Is this anything to do with that van?'

'No.'

'And you're not hurt or in any danger?'

'No.' She stifled another sob.

'Right, then, let's get you home, shall we?'

'Yes, please.' Her voice was small. Home was where she and Josh had once lived. But Josh wasn't there, was he? Just her, all alone in the flat without even a cat to talk to.

She reached for her phone, intending to torture herself further by checking on Flamingo Cam, but realised anew that it was out of charge. Now she couldn't even look at him. It was as though all ties with him were cut and he really was out of her life.

'Will this do?' The driver broke into her thoughts, and she glanced out of the window to see that the car had pulled up alongside the entrance to her flat. Her relief was instantaneous, however she did give the road behind a cautious check to make sure there was no van lurking anywhere.

She got out and dashed to the door, her heart hammering and her keys in her hand. Jamming the key in the lock, she glanced behind to see that the taxi driver was waiting until she was safely inside, and she wished she'd thought to give him a tip. As her door swung open she realised it was too late as, with a wave of his hand, the cab pulled away from the kerb, so she darted into the safety of the hall. Slamming the door firmly shut, she sagged against it for a second before attempting the stairs, her head reeling and her stomach rolling nastily.

Never again, she vowed as she fell onto the sofa. She was never going to touch another drop of alcohol. Ever. Damn Josh. If it wasn't for him and what he'd done, then she would never have got so drunk in the first place.

Sometimes, she positively hated him.

CHAPTER 15

Kit had laughed more tonight than he'd done in a very long time indeed. Angie had been just the tonic he'd needed. They should really try to get together more often (not easy with distance being an issue) because they were really good for each other. They'd met in uni, tried to date, discovered they didn't fancy one another, and settled for being very good friends instead.

As he dropped her off at her hotel with a hug and a kiss on the cheek, he wished, as he'd frequently done over the years, that the pair of them had been attracted to each other. It would have been perfect. But they were friends and nothing more.

Of course Nancy hadn't liked it. He guessed she'd felt threatened by Angie and their bond, but she needn't have been. He'd not had eyes for another woman since the day he'd met her. He'd fallen head over heels in love with her and had still felt the same even after she told him she didn't love him anymore. He guessed that he may love her even now, despite everything. It was hard to shut off his feelings especially when he'd not been the one to apply for a divorce. He'd known they hadn't been getting on too well for a while (more than a while if he was honest) but he'd always assumed they'd work things out.

A van up ahead was signalling it wanted to pull out, and he flashed his lights as he slowed down to let it out. As much as he loved his cottage, he wasn't in any hurry to go home. Not when home was empty and lonely, and there was just him in it. Maybe he should get a cat for company?

What the hell!

A figure darted into the road, waving its arms about, and he instinctively braked. The figure shot up the side of his car, and his mouth dropped open as the rear passenger door was yanked open and a young woman threw herself inside.

'Go!' she commanded.

He swivelled in his seat to look at her. What the hell was she doing in his car? Her face was illuminated by the yellow streetlights and he realised she looked scared. 'Are you OK?'

'No, there's a van, I think it's after me.'

'The van in front?' Kit turned back around to look

at it. The van was trundling up the road, doing possibly fewer than twenty miles an hour. But this was a residential area and there was a primary school up ahead, so twenty was probably the speed limit. He'd not seen any signs to that effect, but as he'd been so deep in thought he'd most likely missed them. Thankfully, he'd not been doing much more than that. At least, he hoped he hadn't. He also hoped there weren't any speed cameras around.

The woman leant forward and peered through the windscreen. 'Yeah, thass it. Can you lose it?'

She really was quite pretty, and he also thought from the way she slurred her words that she might have had too much to drink. Someone should have a word with her about the dangers of too much alcohol and being out on her own at night. Someone should also have a word with her about the danger of leaping into a total stranger's car.

But maybe she had good reason to be as scared as she appeared to be. The driver of the van might well have been bothering her, for all he knew. The only sensible and responsible thing for him to do was to drive her home and make sure she got there safely.

'It's not following us,' Kit pointed out. 'If anything, *we're* following *it*.'

'Then don't,' she said. 'I don't want to follow it. I want to go home.'

'Where is that?'

She let out a sigh and he assumed it was from relief. After all, he could have made her get out. She gave him her address and sank back in the seat, and he saw her shuffling down so just the top half of her head was poking over the sill of the window. He also noticed that she peered out of the side window as he turned right, and her eyes never left the van until it was out of sight. She sighed again.

'Don't worry, I'll make sure you get home safely,' he told her.

She answered with a sob.

'Are you all right?' he asked. My God, what had that van driver done to make her so frightened? 'Do you want me to call the police? I didn't think to make a note of the registration number.'

'My boyfriend left me.' She said and sniffed loudly. 'For a Pink Flamingo.'

'Excuse me?'

'Malaga.'

'Okaaay…' He paused, frowning; she wasn't making a great deal of sense. 'Is this anything to do with that van?'

'No.'

'And you're not hurt or in any danger?'

'No.' She sniffled and swiped at her face. Tears glistened on her cheeks, and Kit hastily turned his attention back to the road.

'Right, then, let's get you home, shall we?' he said. She really was quite drunk.

'Yes, please.' Her voice was small, and his heart went out to her. She looked so frightened as she shrank back into her seat, that a wave of unexpected protectiveness swept over him. She was probably somewhere in her mid to late twenties, he guessed, slender, not very tall, with a heart-shaped face and large eyes which he thought might have been blue, although it was difficult to tell in the light from the streetlamps. Brown hair framed her face, falling in wild curls to below her shoulders. He wanted to look at her some more, but thought he'd better not.

Concentrate on your driving, he told himself. She didn't need him ogling her through the rearview mirror and making her feel even more worried than she already was. She needed to feel secure in the knowledge that this unknown man whose car she'd thrown herself into, would take her home safely. It was the least he could do.

To his surprise, he found he wanted to know more about her. He knew where she lived for instance, but he didn't know her name. Not that he was about to ask. She didn't need that kind of pressure. Any questions on his part could be viewed as him coming on to her, and that was the furthest thing from his mind.

'Will this do?' he asked as he drew to a stop alongside the entrance to her flat, and he heard the jangle of keys as she twisted around to stare out of the rear window.

Then, without a word of thanks (not that he expected any, but it would have been polite considering he'd gone out of his way to take her home) she got out and dashed to the door. He watched her jam the key in the lock and he waited until the door swung open. After glancing around to check for himself that no one was creeping up on her, he gave her a wave and pulled off.

That's my good deed for today, he said to himself as he drove home, feeling pleased he'd been able to help her. But when he parked on his drive and locked his car, he realised she'd left her handbag on the backseat.

It was too late to do anything about it now. He didn't think she'd appreciate him turning up on her doorstep less than half an hour since he'd dropped her off – she might think he was stalking her. But he'd swing by tomorrow and if she wasn't in, he'd pop a note through her letterbox to let her know her bag was safe, and not lost or stolen.

It was only when he'd fallen into bed a half an hour or so later that he realised he'd not thought of

Nancy once this evening, and to his amazement he found he was actually looking forward to seeing the unknown woman again.

CHAPTER 16

Friday mornings weren't meant for hangovers but boy did Esther have a dilly of one. She groaned, and flopped back onto her pillow after squinting at her phone. Miraculously she'd plugged it into the charger last night although she couldn't remember doing so, and she checked to see if there was a text or a missed call from Josh.

Deep down she knew there wasn't going to be, but she still lived in hope. There wasn't – just a weird email from a company called "Fly and Flop" which was clearly a scam, so she deleted it. Oh, and nothing from that firm of landscape gardeners that Dean what's-his-face worked for, either.

She could do with a couple of painkillers, a pint of orange juice, and a bacon sarnie in that order, and she groaned again. It was times like these that she missed Josh the most. He'd always been up for shoving a couple of rashers under the grill and slapping them between two slices of white bread, no matter how many pints he'd had the night before.

Easing herself gingerly upright, Esther tottered into the kitchen in search of some tablets and juice, only to discover that she had neither.

Bugger. And she couldn't find her bag anywhere, either. She must have left it at Charlie's. Actually, she couldn't remember a great deal about last night once the second bottle of wine had been opened. It briefly occurred to her that drinking herself into oblivion didn't actually make her problems go away – the problems were still there in the morning, with an added side of headache and nausea – but she shoved the thought to the side. It was irrelevant since she had no intention of getting drunk again. In fact, she wasn't sure she'd ever drink anything stronger than cola for the foreseeable future.

Things had started to get quite fuzzy as the evening wore on. She recalled laughing a lot, crying even more, and a considerable amount of webcam watching, but the details escaped her. She did remember a van and the taxi, and the feeling of relief when she'd arrived home, but little else.

'Never again,' she muttered, for possibly the fifth time in ten minutes, as she dragged herself into the bathroom. Maybe a shower would help? When she looked in the mirror to check the damage, she flinched. Not only did she look peaky and pasty with sallow skin and dark circles under her eyes, but one side of her face had creases on it from where she'd been sleeping, and the other still held a vague imprint of her laptop keyboard. She did remember something about logging onto Flamingo Cam when she got home, but she must have fallen asleep because she'd woke up with a start a couple of hours later, cramped and cold, her face mashed against the keys. At that point, she'd taken herself off to bed. In fact, she'd hardly managed to undress she realised, because she was still wearing last night's blouse, her underwear, and her socks. At least she'd taken her jeans and pumps off she thought, thankful for small mercies.

A shower went some way to reviving her, as did a hastily drunk coffee, and she was beginning to feel a little more human, until she had a phone call from Charlie that is.

'Please tell me we didn't book a holiday to Malaga last night,' was her friend's opening gambit.

'I don't think so… Oh, shit. Hang on.' Esther's heart sank and she closed her eyes in dismay as a memory floated to the surface of her mind. She opened them again and checked her emails. 'You didn't book it, I did.' She moved the email from spam and back into her inbox. 'I've just spent five-hundred-

and-fifty pounds on a week in Malaga. For two people.'

Charlie let out a groan. 'What? *Really?* When are you going?'

'Um...' Esther hastily scrolled down and grimaced. 'Sunday.'

'*This* Sunday?'

'Yeah. My bank is going to kill me,' Esther said. 'I've gone overdrawn. And I don't even know if I've got enough holiday entitlement.'

'What are you going to do?'

'Plead with my boss?' Esther suggested. 'You wouldn't be able to come with me, would you? I don't fancy going on my own.'

'To plead with your boss?' Charlie sounded surprised.

'No, silly. To Malaga. The holiday is for two people.'

'Sorry, I don't think I'll be able to get the time off either, and if I did Jay wouldn't be too keen on me going away without him considering we're not having a holiday together this year.'

'Fair enough.' She completely understood and wondered if any of her other friends would be up for it instead. She'd better check with the agency first, though. Then she remembered something else. 'I haven't left my bag at yours, have I?'

'Hang on.'

Esther heard Charlie plod around her living room accompanied by an assortment of noises, and she guessed her friend was lifting cushions and peering under the sofa.

'I can't see it,' Charlie replied after a minute or so. 'Are you sure you brought it with you?'

'I definitely did. Damn and blast, I must have left it in the taxi.'

As soon as she got off the phone with Charlie, she checked the 'Appy Cabs app, but there was no sign that she'd ordered a taxi last night. Then she checked her calls, with the same result.

Great. This morning was shaping up to be one of the worst since Josh left her. Not only was she going to be late for work – *again* – and have the added pressure of speaking to the agency and asking for next week off, but she was also going to have to cancel her bank card and report her driver's licence as lost. Not to mention having to spend most of the morning phoning every taxi firm within a ten-mile radius. Her favourite hairbrush was in that bag too, along with most of her makeup. With a sigh, Esther stomped off to work, cursing her ex with every single step.

CHAPTER 17

Kit rang the buzzer, glancing around him as he did so. The building was a three-storey one, with the ground floor being an off-licence, leaving him to assume that the upper storeys were two flats. There were a couple of buzzers, neither of them labelled, so when there wasn't any answer from the one, he tried the other.

He was about to leave and come back another time, when he heard a disembodied voice say, 'Yes?'

'Um, I gave a young lady a lift home last night and she left her bag in my car. I've brought it back.' He held it up, in case there was a camera.

'That must be Esther,' the voice said. 'She's probably at work. You can leave it outside her door – the top floor. It'll be safe enough there. I'd take it, but I can't come to the door because I'm naked.'

'Oh.' Kit blinked. Did he really need to know that?

'Fake tan,' the voice said. 'I've got a cold, so I'm

trying to cheer myself up.'

Right. The cold would explain why he couldn't tell the gender of the voice. It was a bit gruff and nasally.

There was a click and the door opened.

Narrowing his eyes, he stepped inside reluctantly, debating the wisdom of leaving Esther's bag (the voice did say that the woman from last night was called Esther, didn't it?) outside her door, or whether he should call back another time.

Curiosity drove him upstairs and he hesitated outside her flat before knocking, in case she was in and hadn't heard the buzzer. He guessed she was probably suffering from a nasty hangover, so maybe she wasn't even awake yet.

He waited for a minute, listening intently for any sounds from inside the flat, and wasn't sure whether to be relieved or disappointed when the silence stretched out. She clearly wasn't home.

So he propped her bag against the door, and scrabbled about in his jacket pocket for the notepad and pen he always carried. He wrote, **You left this in my car. Hope the hangover wasn't too bad,** and stuffed the note inside so that it was poking out and she'd be sure to see it.

Right then, that was that.

Slowly he descended the stairs, happy in the knowledge that he'd done yet another good deed.

But there was also a tiny little niggle of disappointment that he hadn't managed to see her again.

Stop it, he told himself, as he slid into the car seat and started the engine. This unknown woman might be exceptionally pretty and very cute, but right now he needed to get involved with someone like he needed a hole in the head.

He'd vowed no more relationships, so what was he doing thinking about a girl he'd only met once and knew absolutely nothing about?

Except he now knew her name, didn't he? Esther. Pretty. Just like her.

CHAPTER 18

'You've got three days holiday accrued,' her contact at the staff agency said. 'You'll have to take the other two as unpaid.'

Esther winced. Not only had she paid five-hundred-and fifty-pounds for a holiday she didn't want, but she was going to lose two days' pay that she could ill-afford to lose, plus she'd have to find the spending money for the trip too.

That's that, then, she thought, as she returned to her desk. Decision made. No holiday. And maybe that wasn't such a bad idea, because if she did go to Malaga there was absolutely no way she'd be able to stay away from the Pink Flamingo.

'Do you suffer from a weak bladder?' Sally asked, interrupting her train of thought.

'What?'

'I'm asking because that's the fifth time you've

been to the toilet this morning.'

'Sorry,' Esther said, slipping into her seat and sliding her bag under the desk. 'Women's problems.'

"Stupid idiot problems" would be more accurate. But at least she'd managed to cancel her bank card and arrange for another to be sent to her, and she'd phoned all but two of the taxi firms on her list. And she hadn't clicked on the webcam link once. Although now that the thought had entered her head, she desperately wanted to.

She managed to slip away from her desk once more before lunch to ring the remaining taxi companies, unfortunately without result. It appeared she'd not left her bag in any of their cars or if she had, no one was admitting it. In fact, all of them claimed that she hadn't ordered a taxi from them when she obviously had, and by the time she took her lunch break she was despondent, hungry, still had a headache, and was desperate for her fix of Flamingo Cam. But as usual there was absolutely no activity at all at this time of day.

Sinead hadn't been able to make lunch, so Esther sat at their usual table with a sandwich in front of her and her phone in her hand. This time she was checking in on Cottage Cam. The man who lived there was also nowhere to be seen, which was a pity because she quite enjoyed watching him going about his daily life, doing chores and arguing on his phone.

She was about to take a bite of her sandwich when her phone pinged with a text. It was from Charlie. **Are you going to Malaga?**

No.

That's probably a good thing. You'd only make an idiot of yourself.

Charlie was right. She almost certainly would end up confronting him. Or would beg him to take her back, and the thought of doing either made her cringe with embarrassment.

It was better to chalk it up to experience and leave the wine well alone in the future. Hang on…

What about you and Jay? she texted Charlie.

What about us?

Could you go on holiday? My treat. I'm going to lose the money anyway. You might as well get some benefit from it.

Esther waited a while before Charlie replied**, Are you sure?**

'Positive.

XXXX!!! I love you xxx

Esther smiled. She could almost hear Charlie's squeal of excitement.

Let me know what Jay says asap, and I'll get the name changed on the booking.

I'll pay you back.

You don't have to.

I do!! I want to!! Just don't tell Jay.

On one condition, Esther added.

What? Anything.

Promise me you won't go anywhere near the Pink Flamingo.

Promise! Love U.

LU 2. Speak later.

Esther was smiling as she finished her sandwich, thinking that at least some good was going to come out of the fiasco. Now all she had to do was to find enough money to survive on until the end of the month. She'd start by bringing her own sandwiches to work tomorrow, and she was sure she had a reusable drink bottle somewhere which she could fill with supermarket cola, to save her buying a can. It wouldn't taste as nice as a Pepsi with ice in the cafe, but beggars couldn't be choosers.

With a half-an-hour of her lunchbreak left, she clicked onto Cottage Cam again. The man was conspicuous by his absence, and she spent a few absentminded minutes imagining him following someone or performing some kind of espionage. The details weren't clear, but they involved scaling walls with ropes and wearing black, a bit like Tom Cruise in Mission Impossible Twenty-Six, or whatever the latest MI film was called. Josh used to love those type of films she thought sorrowfully, before pushing him to the back of her mind.

She studied the outside of the house again, looking for clues of where it might be.

There wasn't a lot to go on. It appeared to be an older building, constructed out of stone rather than the red brick that the new builds which were prevalent in Worcester's outskirts were made of. She wasn't sure why, but she thought the cottage might be in one of the villages surrounding the city.

Then she gave a snort. Who was she kidding? The house could be anywhere in the world, although it did look quintessentially English, and country-village English at that. She couldn't see much of the garden except for a reflection of bushes, lots of flowers, and a table and some chairs in the glass of the French doors. Not much to go on was it? But she had a feeling…

Anyway, enough of that. She'd perved at the poor guy's house enough for one day and it was time for her to get back to work.

With a final check of her emails (still nothing from the landscape gardening company) she popped her phone in her bag and trundled back to the bank for another afternoon of boredom.

She did have one piece of good news and a bit of excitement, she discovered later, when she arrived home.

Two really, although the second one was a bit creepy. The first was an email from LandScape Ltd inviting her to an interview next Tuesday. She'd have to take the morning off but it would be worth it if she did actually get the job. And she found she badly wanted this job, despite not knowing much about either what it entailed or the company. It would be nice to work in the same place and for the same firm for a while, and to not be constantly wondering whether the job she was currently doing would still be available next week. The excitement and buzz of meeting new people and working in new places every few days/weeks/months had imperceptibly worn off, and she had a need for something more permanent and predictable.

The second piece of good news, and the one that she thought was a bit creepy, was discovering her handbag propped up against the door of her flat. Not the outside door – the one leading to the street – but the inside one, at the top of the stairs.

There was a hand-written note stuffed just inside so it was poking out. **You left this in my car. Hope the hangover wasn't too bad.**

Oh, my God. Whoever had left it here knew where she lived.

Esther hyperventilated for a moment before she

realised that of course the person knew where she lived – she'd given the taxi driver her address, for goodness sake!

She checked the contents, and when nothing appeared to be missing she sent a silent "thank you" to the man in question. She felt guilty. Not only had she not tipped the poor driver, but she'd left her bag in his car and he'd had the decency to return it to her. If she ever discovered which firm he worked for, she'd make sure to pay him what she owed him and give him a decent tip.

Feeling more settled and a little more in control with the Malaga holiday fiasco sorted, an interview to look forward to, and her bag in her possession once more, she decided to make some dinner before she began researching LandScape Ltd.

Rather than switching on the TV – a habit she'd taken to doing since Josh had left because the flat was too quiet and empty without him and at least the TV was company of sorts – she brought her laptop into the kitchen with her while she went about preparing a hot meal. It was only pasta and cheese, with some frozen broccoli thrown in for good measure, nothing fancy, but at least it was home-cooked and not out of a box and microwaved.

As she worked, she clicked on Flamingo Cam as usual, but the cleaners weren't doing anything exciting so she flipped onto Cottage Cam instead.

For a second she thought the house was empty, then she spotted him in the kitchen, partially out of sight. He had his back to her and his shoulders were jiggling a bit and she wondered what he was doing until she realised he was standing in front of the hob, cooking.

Watching him stir something in a pan at exactly the same time as she was stirring her pasta in her own pan, made her feel as though they were in the same room, cooking together, side-by-side. It was quite surreal but rather comforting, and for the first time since Josh walked out on her, she didn't feel quite so alone.

She continued to watch as he sat at the table to eat his meal at exactly the same time that she sat at hers, and her fascination continued as they washed up together, and didn't end even when he left the room. If anything, it increased when he appeared in his bedroom and proceeded to take his shirt off.

Her eyes widened and her heart gave a little skip excitement when she saw the flatness of his stomach and width of his shoulders. But her attention was really caught by his chest and she leant forward for a closer look, wishing there was a zoom facility. She urgently wanted a close-up of those pecs.

Oh yum.

She knew she should stop watching, but what woman in her right mind would be able to switch off now?

She certainly couldn't.

Thankfully, he did it for her.

With one swift movement the man drew the curtains, leaving Esther staring at the blank face of a shuttered window. It also left her with a new obsession and one that was a strong contender for Josh and Flamingo Cam.

She wasn't entirely sure whether that was a good thing or not.

CHAPTER 19

Esther dressed with considerable care on Tuesday morning, even going as far as to iron her blouse, because she wanted to make the best possible impression. She'd done some research online last night and was surprised to discover that LandScape Ltd had a glossy and professional website, and if the testimonials were to be believed, they'd had some fairly large and impressive commissions.

She'd even tried to do a bit of swatting up on gardening terms, but it was quite a large field (she'd chuckled over the pun), and to be honest, they wouldn't be hiring her for her green fingers or her ability to tell a pagoda from a pergola. There *was* something that had given her a bit of a pause, though. Dean Reynolds was the owner of the company and not merely an employee, as he'd led her to believe.

If she got the job, she would be *his* PA. Boy was

she glad that she'd not been romantically attracted to him. She suspected she'd have felt the same way even if she wasn't still feeling so sore and bruised because of Josh. The spark simply hadn't been there. Dean was good-looking, but…

Now the man on Cottage Cam, on the other hand... yum.

Especially when she'd seen what was under his clothes. The top-half, she amended, putting the finishing touches to her make-up and blending like mad. She wanted to look well-put-together, but not so overdone that she looked as though she was off to a nightclub. Professional, not sultry, was the aim.

Stepping back, she eyed herself critically. Her hair was in a bun, her make-up was barely there, and her suit was smart, the blouse not too revealing. All she needed was a pair of heels and she was ready.

Satisfied that she'd done the best she could with what was available, she grabbed her bag and headed out of the door.

Middlewick was a pretty village about fifteen miles from Worcester and surrounded by rolling fields and lush hedgerows. LandScape Ltd was situated on the other side of the village, and as she drove through it she all but drooled over the chocolate-box, butter-coloured, stone houses, with their colourful window-boxes and thatched roofs. The village itself boasted a pub, a little shop, a green with a duck pond, and a view of the distant Malvern Hills if the angle was right and it wasn't too hazy.

Esther pulled into the driveway of a converted barn, switched off the engine and took a deep breath. She'd arrived. Of course, it had helped that she'd done the virtual journey online beforehand, so she'd known exactly where she was going and how to get there. She might still be an emotional mess, but no one could accuse her of being unprepared or disorganised.

Another deep breath, followed by a quick check in the rearview mirror to make sure her lipstick was still in place, and she was as ready as she would ever be.

Dean met her at the door. 'Esther, nice to see you again. You found us OK?'

She nodded. 'I wouldn't be much of a PA if I hadn't,' she replied with a bright smile.

'Touché. But you'd be surprised how many people can't.'

'Why are you based here, if that's the case?' she wanted to know, as he showed her into a spacious office, which was bright and airy with floor to ceiling windows on three sides.

'You're thinking that the company would be better off if it was nearer the city or the motorway?'

'Maybe. I can see the attraction of this place

though.' Esther gazed out of the windows at the beautiful garden beyond. 'You're selling a dream, a lifestyle,' she observed.

'That, and the fact that we didn't have to buy the property. The barn is part of my parents' farm and the rent is non-existent.'

'Ah!' That explained it.

'Right. Take a seat and let's get down to business,' Dean said.

For the next half-hour he grilled her very thoroughly indeed, before leaning back in his chair and nodding thoughtfully. 'Do you think you can work with me?' he asked.

'I don't see why not. I've worked with hundreds of people.' It was no exaggeration. 'I'm flexible and adaptable, and nothing much fazes me. If I were to be offered the job, it wouldn't take me long to fall into your way of working.'

'This is a small outfit. Just me, my brother, and another designer. Neither of them is in the office much, so you won't have a great deal to do with them. I'm more of a front of house person, so it's me you'll be dealing with for the most part. We outsource the dirty stuff, although we do have a resident plantsman, but you probably won't see much of him, either. Basically, I need someone in the office who can do everything from answering the phones, to coordinating teams of workmen, to making high-spending clients feel they are the most important people in the world. Oh, and if you could feed the cat and make the occasional cup of tea, it wouldn't go amiss.'

She gave him a polished professional smile and asked, 'Would that be Rooibos, or fruit? Earl Grey or Darjeeling?'

Dean laughed. He was a nice man, she realised, and there was something about him that reminded her of...? Nope, it was gone. It would come to her eventually. Not that it mattered. She seriously did think she could work for him. LandScape Ltd might be out in the sticks and she had a feeling that she'd be left to her own devices most of the time, but it would give her a chance to prove to Dean and to herself that she could keep the nuts and bolts of the company running smoothly, leaving the designers to get on with what they did best.

There was silence for a moment, a silence which Esther desperately wanted to fill but didn't. Instead she sat quietly, without fidgeting, allowing him to make his mind up about her. From experience, she knew that if he wanted her he'd most likely offer her the job there and then. If he didn't or was uncertain, he'd tell her he'd let her know. She'd lost count of the number of times she'd lived through the exact same scenario.

'If I were to offer you the job on a trial basis of a month, what would you say?' he asked eventually,

'I'd say yes.' A trial basis sounded reasonable on his part and, as for her, if it didn't work out she could always go back to temping.

'When can you start?' he asked.

In reality she could have started tomorrow, but morally it wouldn't be right. She wanted to give the agency enough time to find a replacement temp for the bank, so she said, 'Next Monday?'

Dean leant across the desk and held out his hand. Esther shook it.

'Monday, it is. Depending on satisfactory references,' he added.

'Of course.' Esther expected nothing less.

Managing to hold herself together as she said goodbye, she walked to her car and got in. She even managed to keep some semblance of control as the car trundled down the drive and pulled out onto the road running through the village.

But when she saw a layby she drove into it, switched the engine off, and let out a squeal of excitement. She'd done it! She'd got the job. Esther bounced up and down in the seat, slapping the steering wheel and giggling like a fool. She'd grab a bottle of wine on the way home and maybe they'd have a takeaway tonight to celebrate. Indian sounded good and it was ages since she'd had a chicken madras.

It was only when she reached for her phone to share her good news with Josh that she remembered that she'd have to drink the wine by herself, and the chicken madras would be eaten alone in front of the TV. Her jubilant mood subsided.

Damn Josh and his selfish, hard heart.

CHAPTER 20

What was wrong with him? Kit wondered. He had an image of a woman with bouncing brown curls and large blue eyes stuck in his head, and he couldn't seem to shift it. It had been there since he'd inadvertently picked Esther up and given her a lift home. He knew he was being daft (as she probably already had a husband or boyfriend) and rather reckless. He was, after all, still married and had vowed never to get involved with anyone again, but she kept popping into his thoughts when he was least expecting it, and he found it extremely disconcerting.

Being an adult, he was perfectly capable of not acting on wild impulses and sudden urges, and the fact that he wanted to see her again (he told himself it was to check that she was OK), was something he could easily control and not give in to. The itch was nothing more than animal attraction and one he needn't scratch. A relationship was surplus to requirements and would only be trouble. Although he did find some consolation in his healthy male reaction to a pretty woman – it proved he was recovering from the battering Nancy had given his heart. And maybe "never" was a long time. He'd amend that to "one day". But not anytime soon, he vowed.

Which was why he was having difficulty understanding the impulse that had made him drive to the nearest florist, purchase a large and quite sumptuous bouquet, and then drive to Esther's flat and press the buzzer.

Once again there was no answer. He'd been hoping she was in; it was early evening and he'd been counting on the fact that she might have got home from work by now. Which was a silly assumption, considering he had no idea where she worked or what job she did. She might work shifts or unsociable hours. Or, and his heart sank a little at the thought, she might be out to dinner with someone, a *special* someone, so it was probably best if he just left the flowers here, with the card he'd already written on in the event that she was out.

Kit double-checked what he'd written.

Hope you got your bag back ok. If you fancy going out for a coffee or a drink, give me a call.

He'd added his mobile number underneath. The

ball was now in her park. She must realise that he was a decent guy to have given her a lift home the other night. He wasn't some stalker, although he was beginning to feel a bit like one and he felt sure the woman (her cold had cleared enough for him to tell the voice's gender as she let him in through the main door once again) in the flat below Esther's might be starting to think of him in that light. He'd be surprised if she let him in again the next time he called.

Not that there would be a next time. It was now up to Esther. If she was interested, she'd phone him.

He just hoped he wasn't stepping on any guy's toes by leaving her a bouquet. He didn't want to get her into trouble, but what else was he supposed to do?

The thought of loitering about outside her flat and waiting for her to return home crossed his mind but he dismissed it immediately as not being a sensible thing to do.

It was better this way. Everyone loved flowers and a bouquet was quite non-threatening, as was the message on the card.

He'd wait to hear from her.

If he ever did.

If not, the odds were that he'd never see her again and that would be that. At least he'd tried.

CHAPTER 21

Esther had been for a swim. It wasn't the kind of thing she did often, but the thought of another evening sitting at home watching a boxset all by herself was making her feel quite down. So she'd gone to the leisure centre instead. It was ladies' night in the pool and considering she didn't fancy strutting her stuff in front of a load of men and the gym had never appealed to her, she decided to give it a go.

To her surprise, she'd quite enjoyed herself and felt rather virtuous afterwards, as though she'd earned her meagre supper of beans on toast. For the first time in ages she was feeling relaxed. Not happy, not yet – she guessed she'd have a while to go before she could describe herself as happy – but she was getting there. She was no longer a mess, and she was gradually finding a degree of contentment and was even looking forward to what the future would bring.

When she unlocked the outside door to the flat and walked up the stairs, she saw something that stopped her in her tracks.

Propped against her door was a bunch of flowers. Not a bunch, exactly. More of a bouquet. Quite a large bouquet and a very pretty one at that. She picked it up and was about to take it to the flat above – people sometimes got the two mixed up and it wouldn't be the first time she had received a delivery meant for upstairs, or vice versa – when she paused. Maybe this was for her after all? Her heart missed a beat at the thought.

They must be from Josh. Thank God! He'd seen the error of his ways and this was his way of saying he was sorry. Fingers shaking slightly, she searched for a card. When she found it her heart missed another beat, but this time it wasn't because of excitement or hope.

The card read, Hope you got your bag back ok. If you fancy going out for a coffee or a drink, give me a call.

A mobile number, one she didn't recognise, was written underneath.

Hastily, she glanced back down the stairs as if she expected the flower sender to be lurking at the bottom of them, waiting to pounce.

The staircase was empty, but that didn't make her

feel any better. Tentatively she put the key in the lock and slowly eased open the door to her flat, half expecting the taxi driver to be lurking on the other side.

The flat also appeared to be empty.

Esther quickly stepped inside, slammed the door shut, then slid the bolt across. She realised she was trembling, and she dumped the bouquet in the tiny kitchen wishing she'd never picked it up.

At first, she'd been delighted that the driver had been honest enough to return her bag. Now, though, she was beginning to wish he'd kept it. A part of her hoped he was just being nice. Another part of her wondered if she'd acquired a stalker.

'Thanks, Josh,' she grumbled. This was all his fault. If he'd still been living here, a strange guy wouldn't have dared leave flowers on her doorstep. If Josh hadn't buggered off, then she wouldn't have gone to Charlie's in the first place that night. Neither would she have got hammered, nor would she have booked a bloody holiday to bloody Malaga, that she hadn't even been able to go on.

OK, not being able to go had actually been a godsend because if she had gone, she wouldn't have been able to attend the interview, and she felt all warm and excited whenever she thought about her new job. But it still rankled that she'd been silly enough to book it in the first place.

Thinking about Malaga had Esther heading straight for her laptop, and while she waited for her toast to pop and her beans to start bubbling, she clicked onto Flamingo Cam.

The night was young in Pink Flamingo terms, but already the place was fairly full, and she could see Josh behind the bar, looking all summery in a Hawaiian shirt. He looked good with a tan, she conceded, grudgingly. It was probably real by now and not sprayed on, considering he'd been over there for more than a month.

She was about to butter her toast, when Josh did something that made her gasp in horror.

He walked out from behind the bar, giving her the opportunity to stare at his brown legs poking out from a pair of tight denim cut-offs, strode up to a girl who was wearing the tiniest pair of shorts in the world and a bright blue boob tube, grabbed hold of her and put his arms around her waist. The girl melted into him as if she belonged in his arms, and when he kissed her passionately, Esther let out a strangled cry, tears springing to her eyes.

Not only that, but to add insult to enormous injury, when the pair of them broke apart, Josh stared directly into the camera and gave a little wave. Esther shrank back, appalled.

Bloody hell, it was as if he knew she was watching him.

Mortified, she felt her cheeks grow hot; he definitely knew she was there, the bastard. And he was enjoying rubbing her nose in it. How did he—?

Charlie! Grabbing her phone, Esther clicked on her friend's number. The call went straight to answerphone. Furious and feeling more than a little betrayed, she sent her a text instead.

Josh knows about me watching him. How could you???

Appetite gone, she scraped the beans into the bin, swiftly followed by the toast, before allowing herself to look at Flamingo Cam again.

The bastard was all over the girl, his hands running up and down her back and underneath the skinny top. His eyes were open though, and his gaze was on the camera, knowing exactly what he was doing and how much it would hurt her.

Esther felt sick.

She wondered how often he'd stood in the middle of the bar, playing tongue-tonsils with this girl or that, before Esther had tuned in and finally caught him at it.

She checked her phone.

Sorry, Charlie's text said. **Jay let it slip**

I asked you NOT to go there!!

She didn't wait for a reply. Instead she turned off her mobile and threw it across the counter. What the hell had Charlie been thinking? Now Josh knew exactly how much she'd been pining after him, like a love-sick teenager with a crush on a pop star.

He must be laughing his head off.

She wanted to curl up and die. Feeling almost as low as when he'd first left, she sank onto the sofa, clutched a cushion to her chest and bawled. While Josh had his hands on any girl within grabbing distance, Esther had never felt so alone in her life.

The only bloke who'd shown any kind of interest in her lately was a stalker taxi driver. The way she felt right at this moment, she might even give him a call if it meant easing this crushing loneliness.

Feeling desolate, she crawled into bed, and cried herself to sleep.

CHAPTER 22

Arguing with Dean wasn't a particularly good start to a Monday morning, but dammit, his brother was being unreasonable. He was refusing to buy his share of the business from him until there was more of an indication of what Nancy's settlement might be.

Kit wanted to start the ball rolling now – if Dean owned all of LandScape Ltd, then Nancy couldn't get her grasping hands on any of it. He'd planned on giving her 100 per cent of what he realised from the sale, if she agreed not to demand half the house.

He thought that was fair. Dean, however, didn't agree with him. 'But what does this new lawyer say?' he kept asking.

'Nothing, and that's my point.' Kit sighed in exasperation. 'I've not heard a peep out of him.'

'Give him a call,' Dean said, using his reasonable voice, the one which had a tendency to rile Kit even more.

'I have. He said he'll contact me when he's got something concrete to report.'

'Well, then.'

'I want to get things sorted,' he growled. 'I don't know how much longer I can live in this limbo. It's the not-knowing that's driving me to distraction.'

'You don't say.' Dean raised his eyebrows.

'Oh, for goodness' sake!' he exclaimed. 'I can't talk any sense into you.'

'That's because you're the one not making any sense,' Dean retorted. 'I know it's been dragging on for weeks, but these things take time. That's the problem with you, you've not got any patience, you always want things done yesterday. Or sooner.'

'Yeah? Well, you need to be a bit more proactive. You're too laid back for your own good.'

'That's why we make such a good team,' Dean came back with.

Kit took a deep breath – Dean simply wasn't getting it. If they didn't have a plan in place, then Nancy might cock everything up. The solution he'd arrived at in the wee small hours last night wasn't ideal, but at least it meant he'd get to keep his house, and although he wouldn't be a partner in LandScape, he could continue to work there. At the moment however, the last thing he felt like doing was working for his brother and having Dean as his boss. He'd be insufferable. Just like he was being now. He wasn't even willing to contemplate the idea, let alone start crunching some numbers.

'I give up,' Kit said, throwing his hands in the air.

'Good,' Dean fired back. 'We'll talk some more when we know what's what. I need to get on, our PA is starting today.'

'What PA?'

'We discussed it, remember? We agreed we needed admin support in the office if the business is to grow.'

'If we don't sort out Nancy, the only thing we'll be growing is weeds,' Kit muttered darkly, before stalking out of the office and into the reception area.

For God's sake, why couldn't Dean see that this was the best solution all round?

He heard his brother's footsteps following him, but he was done talking for now. He had a client to see, and he needed to get rid of some of his frustration before the meeting, else he was in danger of suggesting they crazy pave their garden and be done with it. He felt like someone had crazy paved his whole life and had added a grotesque folly in the middle of it for good measure.

He yanked open the main door and stormed through it. When he heard a startled squeak, he sent the resident cat a silent apology as he marched toward his car, pressing the key fob crossly. His hasty departure down the drive sent a spray of gravel skittering across the lawn, but darn it, he had a right to be upset.

They'd speak again later he promised himself, but right now he needed to focus on the job he was heading off to. Which was why he became even more unhappy when his thoughts turned to a certain woman who had failed to call him. Why was he even thinking about her? She clearly wasn't interested, and it wasn't as if he wanted to start a relationship with anyone right now, was it? It didn't stop him from feeling glum though and even the thought of Angie coming around for lunch later, didn't lift his mood. She would be flying back to California soon, and suddenly Kit felt as though everyone was deserting him.

He shook his head. From now on he'd stick to plants. You knew where you were with a hebe or a geranium.

CHAPTER 23

Esther simply knew she was going to love working at LandScape Ltd. Who could fail to be seduced by such a pretty village and by such beautiful surroundings? As she drove through Middlewick and out the other side towards the converted barn, she glanced around with envy. She'd kill to live in a place like this, she thought, going as slow as she dared in order to admire the view. The last time she'd come this way, she'd been too nervous to take it all in, but she was early for her first day (Esther hated being late) and she had time to admire the scenery.

And such gorgeous scenery it was! She especially liked the cottages with the thatched roofs, although she wasn't sure she would want to live in one herself, and she shuddered as she imagined all the creatures that might have made their homes in the thatch. But the houses with the red tiled roofs were just as delightful. No two cottages were the same, she noticed; each one had their own character and style and was surrounded by flowers and greenery. She had no idea what the plants and shrubs were, although she suspected she might discover their names if the month trial period worked out. For today, all she knew was that they were pretty, and that the sun was shining, and she was feeling happier than she'd done since Josh had dropped his bombshell.

Ooh, look at the pretty names: Primrose Cottage, Duck Pond Drive, Wildflower Lane… She especially liked the last one, because as she drove past it she could see the nodding heads of hundreds of flowers along the verges and dotted in the hedgerows. With a sigh of contentment, she pulled into the entrance to LandScape Ltd and parked alongside a sleek, black car.

'Right, here goes,' she muttered, grabbing her handbag off the passenger seat, and checking that none of the buttons of her blouse had come undone. Satisfied, she strode toward the door and was about to open it, her hand on the handle, when she hesitated, hearing raised voices coming from inside.

Then without warning the door was wrenched open and with a squeak, Esther was pulled off balance and she toppled sideways, landing on her backside in one of the planters which sat either side of the entrance. By the time she'd extricated herself, brushing frantically at the seat of her trousers to dislodge any dirt clinging to them, whoever had knocked her over had got into the black car and was rapidly barrelling down the drive.

To her dismay, when she looked back at the door it was to find Dean standing there, a witness to her embarrassment and wearing a long-suffering look on his face.

'I see you've met my brother,' he said dryly.

If you could call being knocked over by a bloke who hadn't had the decency to stop to check that she was OK, "met", she thought, then she supposed she had. And she didn't particularly want to meet him again, either. Not if she could help it.

'Don't mind him. He can be a bit, shall we say… volatile on occasion,' her new boss said.

Esther smiled to show there was no harm done and followed him inside. Thank God she would be working for this brother and not the other one, she thought, with a last pat at her bottom.

Dean proceeded to give her a guided tour of the converted barn.

'This is your desk,' he said, pointing, and Esther gave her workstation a quick once-over, seeing nothing to give her pause, so she dropped her bag on her chair and nodded.

Dean's office was already familiar to her, and there was another office which must be his brother's plus a few other offices and storerooms. She was surprised to see there was another wing to the barn where Dean lived. The building was an L-shape, with the longer side housing the various company offices and the shorter part being a one-bedroomed apartment, he explained. There was also a sleek geometrically designed garden which she suspected was for Dean's personal use, constructed of steel and concrete with darkly gleaming polished wooden seating and strategically placed enormous stone pots. In addition, there was a small kitchen and a cloakroom for staff behind the main reception area, and she made a note to check out what was stocked in the cupboards, because part of her remit would be coffee and tea making, both for her boss and for his clients.

After the initial tour, he left her to settle in at her desk and familiarise herself with the phone lines and the computer system. The databases took a little longer, but by the end of the morning, Esther had a grip on both the ordering and invoicing systems (she'd used the same programme while working for a couple of other companies) and could find her way around the filing system.

When she finally stopped for lunch, she took her foil packet of sandwiches into the kitchen to sit at the table to eat them. The cat that Dean had mentioned put in an appearance, winding itself around her legs until she gave in to its mewing, found a pouch of salmon and tuna cat food and popped it in the bowl.

The cat immediately turned its attention to the food and totally ignored her. Typical.

She sat back down, bit into her sandwich, and took the opportunity to scroll through her phone, having not even thought about it once since she'd arrived because she'd simply been too busy. She preferred it that way. She hated being bored, but the break from her duties was more than welcome, and as she chomped her way through a couple of cheese and pickle sandwiches, she clicked on Cottage Cam.

Her screen showed the sun shining directly on the back of the house, and the French doors were wide open, allowing her to see right inside. She realised the living room must run the full length of the house as she spied the glint of a window at the far end of the room. A shape was moving inside the kitchen and she assumed it was the man himself, but after a while when nothing much had happened she gave in to the urge to check on Flamingo Cam.

To her consternation, instead of it being angled toward the bar, the camera showed a rather dingy ceiling. Great. Either it had been accidentally knocked or someone had altered the angle. Disgruntled, she got up and made a coffee, but when she looked at her phone screen again, to her surprise it was back on Cottage Cam.

She tilted the screen for a better look and her eyes widened. Was that a woman? It was. Esther could see part of a blond head, the hair cut into a chic bob, and the curve of a cream-bloused shoulder. The woman moved, giving Esther a better view.

She still couldn't see her properly but as she turned, Esther could clearly see the top she was wearing. It was a blouse, with a riffle down the front, and it looked classy and expensive. She wondered where the woman had bought it, because she would dearly love to have one just like it.

Was the woman his wife, she wondered, or his girlfriend? Disappointment coursed through her, although she knew she'd never ever get to meet Cottage Cam Man. Even if the property was somewhere in England – and she was convinced it was – it could be absolutely anywhere in the country.

Yet she couldn't help feeling betrayed and more than a little put out to think he was already taken. She'd been quite enjoying her little fantasies about him, but it seemed he was nothing more than an ordinary guy living an ordinary life. As well as a wife or girlfriend, he could have two point four kids and a dog tucked away in that little cottage of his. She hadn't seen any evidence of children or pets, but she'd been watching him for a few weeks now and she'd only just noticed the woman, so anything was possible.

Feeling slightly deflated, Esther finished her lunch and returned to her desk, thinking that it was about time she stopped living vicariously through her screen and began to live life for herself. Forget Josh, forget the man in the cottage.

She had her own life to lead and she needed to start living it.

CHAPTER 24

Esther had a date, a bona fide, honest to goodness date with a real man. She was going out to dinner tonight with a guy she'd never met before. It was a blind date, but a date nevertheless, and one she was both looking forward to and was immensely nervous about.

Despite her vow, she had been on the internet again, but not for voyeuristic purposes this time. Two nights ago she'd signed up to a dating site and within a day had been approached by no fewer than six men, all of them "anxious" to meet her.

She hadn't liked the look of, or the sound of five of them. One of them was interested in a good time, which she guessed was a euphemism for no-strings sex. Another WLTM the woman of his dreams, so no pressure there, then. The third was possibly older than her dad, although it was difficult to tell because he'd inexpertly Photoshopped his image and it was rather blurry. The fourth guy was pictured in a pair of extremely short shorts, leaving little to the imagination, and the fifth was really, *really* into model aircraft and drones. She had visions of him discovering where she lived and sending a drone to spy on her through her window.

The sixth, though, seemed positively normal. The photo hadn't been tampered with – she hoped – and his bio said that he enjoyed eating out, long walks on the beach, and running marathons. Esther translated the last into the hope that he was relatively fit, in both senses of the word. She liked eating out, too; it beat having to cook hands down. She also quite enjoyed the odd walk on the beach if it was warm and sunny, and although she'd never run a marathon in her life she was quite happy for her potential other half to run them, if that's what he was in to. Besides, opposites were supposed to attract, and it was healthy to have separate interests, wasn't it?

She decided to wear a black jumpsuit which wasn't too tight or clingy, because she didn't want to give her date the wrong impression, and her best black stilettos. Because she was meeting Giles at the restaurant, she didn't think her four-inch heels would be a problem as she didn't anticipate having to make a run for it. As keen as she was, she was also being cautious and sensible, because she'd texted Charlie to let her friend know where she was going, just in case.

Satisfied that she'd ticked all the boxes, she headed out of the door and got into the taxi she'd ordered. There was no way she was going to risk damaging her gorgeous shoes by walking into town, so she had decided to treat herself.

This particular driver was a woman, so it wasn't the driver who'd brought her home a few weeks ago, and Esther was rather relieved. Since receiving the flowers, she hadn't heard so much as a peep out of him and she wasn't sure she wanted to. She did still have his number, even though she had no idea why she'd kept it. Maybe she'd had a vague notion of being able to use it as evidence if the man turned out to be a stalker after all. Or maybe she knew she'd become desperate enough to give him a call and take him up on his offer of coffee.

'This will do,' she said to the driver, and she got out at the bottom end of town near Friar Street. It wasn't far, so she'd walk the rest of the way. There was a fabulous Argentinian restaurant halfway along the road, and that was where she was meeting her date. She hoped she'd be able to recognise him.

Cheeks slightly pink with embarrassment and feeling that everyone could tell she was on a blind date, Esther almost slunk in through the door, and peered around the restaurant.

Ah, that must be him. A man was sitting on his own at a table, a glass of red wine in front of him, busily shredding a napkin. She let out a slow breath, glad to see that he looked like his photo (more-or-less) and that he was possibly as nervous as she was.

'Giles?' she asked, approaching the table and hoping that he liked what he saw enough to actually admit to being Giles. For a fleeting second, she had the awful feeling that he might deny it and was relieved when he stood up and nodded.

'You must be Esther,' he said looking her up and down. 'You look great.'

'Thanks.' She felt great too, the heels giving her height as well as confidence, and she felt a million dollars in them.

He didn't look too bad, either. Possibly a little older than she'd been expecting – she'd put his age at thirty-five – but she suspected he could be at least five years older than that. She wasn't bothered, though.

Giles was good company, funny and entertaining, and the food was fantastic, so all-in-all, Esther rated the evening a success. There was one little thing that bothered her, though. He kept checking the time, glancing down at the large silver watch on his wrist, and on one occasion he looked at his phone and made a face. It crossed her mind that perhaps he wasn't having as good a time as she was, and was hoping he could escape soon.

At about ten-thirty they said their goodbyes on the pavement outside the restaurant, after exchanging phone numbers, her taxi idling at the kerb as he gave her a quick peck on the cheek. She wasn't entirely certain she wanted to go on another date with him, but she wasn't averse to it, either. There hadn't been an instant spark of attraction on her part, but it was early days yet and she was still reeling from Josh, so she decided to give him a chance if he called her again. He might not (the peck on the cheek was hardly knicker-fizzing stuff) but maybe he was being a gentleman and not rushing her.

She sent a text Charlie on the way home to tell her how it went and reassure her friend that she'd not been abducted.

Glad he's not a minger, Charlie replied. **Send me a photo**.

Esther was about to text that she didn't have one, when she remembered the dating site. By the time the taxi pulled up outside her flat, Esther had downloaded his image from the site and pinged it out to Charlie with the caption, **He's a bit older in real life!**

How old? came the instant reply.

Esther checked that her door was securely locked and dropped her keys on the coffee table, then went to change into her pyjamas.

About thirty-five, give or take.

He's not an old-age pensioner, then? Ha, ha.

No.

Where does he live?

Droitwich.

Not too far away if you want to see him again, but far enough so you won't bump into him if you nip out for a loaf of bread, Charlie pointed out.

Esther ended the conversation with a smiley face emoji, then she took her make-up off and climbed into bed.

For the first time since Josh had left, Esther didn't find the bed too big or the flat too empty. Giles might not be The One, but at least she'd proved to herself that she could dip her toe in the dating game water without getting it bitten off. The last thing she wanted was a rebound romance, but there was nothing to stop her from having a bit of fun while she waited for her heart to recover.

She made the decision that if he did give her a call and asked her out, she'd go, and with that she dropped off to sleep without even thinking about Flamingo Cam, for once.

CHAPTER 25

'Oh, no. I didn't, did I?' Kit put a hand to his mouth.

'You did,' Dean said. 'You knocked her straight into the planter.'

His brother was smiling, so it couldn't have been too bad, but still… 'Is she all right? I didn't injure her, did I?'

He reached for his pint and took a deep gulp. The pair of them were in the Willow and Wicket enjoying a swift drink before a bar meal. Sometimes the pub was the best place to meet for a catch up, as they both had to eat and neither of them wanted to spend the evening at the office.

'She's fine,' Dean reassured him.

'Thank God for that! I thought I heard a noise, but I assumed it was the cat. How is your Girl Friday working out?'

'Really well. You'll like her. She's a fast learner,

efficient, uses her own initiative, just gets on with things without any fuss. She's friendly and professional with the contractors and the clients—'

Kit couldn't resist jumping in. 'You like her, don't you?'

'Yes, she's— Hang on a minute, are you suggesting that I *like* her?'

'Don't you?' Kit tried to hold back a smirk and failed. His brother was picky when it came to women and it was rare for him to show an interest, despite the number of first dates he went on.

'Actually, no. Not in the sense you mean. Although, I did meet her on a sort of blind date. Steve invited me out for drinks with some of his friends, and she was there. I got the feeling that she wasn't exactly attracted to me, either.'

'That's probably a good thing, considering she now works for you.'

'For us,' Dean said. 'She works for *us*.'

'I'm not sure if there'll be an "us" if Nancy gets her way.' Kit's mood abruptly darkened

'Don't start this again. I told you before, you need to wait to hear back from your solicitor before you make any rash decisions.'

'It's not rash. It's called thinking ahead and planning for any and all contingencies.'

'I'm *not* buying you out,' his brother said, yet again.

'You seem to forget that the business hasn't got the funds.'

'You can raise a loan—'

'No!' Dean slapped a hand down on the bar. The noise level dropped a couple of decibels and he looked around, giving everyone a sheepish smile.

Kit blinked. It wasn't like his brother to lose his temper, even if it had only been for a second, and it spoke volumes. It told him that Dean was more worried about the situation than he was letting on. Which made Kit even more determined to get some figures together and put a plan in place. Just in case the worst should happen.

Because he had an awful feeling that it just might.

CHAPTER 26

For a small company, LandScape Ltd was quite busy, Esther thought, and this morning was no exception. Dean had a couple booked in for eleven o'clock to go over some revised plans for their very extensive garden, Esther had a stack of invoices to prepare for payment, there was a JCB that couldn't get down a path between two houses because the company they used had sent the wrong size, and the phone hadn't stopped ringing.

'Good morning, LandScape Ltd. How can I help?'

'You're the new girl?' The voice was male and gruff, and more than a little rude.

'Yes, I am. How can I help?' She kept her tone friendly and polite – there was no way she was going to let some contractor ruffle her feathers.

'I'm christian,' the caller said, and she sighed. She hoped the man wasn't about to try to engage her in conversation about religion, because she had far too much to do today. 'I'm sorry, I'm not very religious,' she said. 'Is there anything else I can help you with?'

'Just how new are you?'

Cheeky git, she thought. 'This is my…' she counted them off in her head, 'seventh day.'

'And you don't know who I am yet?'

She bit her lip, hoping she hadn't offended a client, but to be fair, she couldn't be expected to know everyone in such a short space of time. 'No, sorry. Dean's probably mentioned you but there's such a lot to take in,' she began, not wanting to land her employer in the proverbial manure by admitting that he'd not brought her attention to this strange man on the other end of the phone.

'I'm Dean's brother.'

His broth—? 'Ah, you're *Kit*.' Oh my God, she felt such a fool. Kit… Kris… *Kristian*…? She should have made the connection.

'So, he has mentioned me?'

'Of course he has. You're one of LandScape's designers.'

'And the rest,' he muttered. At least, that's what she thought he'd said.

'Did you want to speak to Dean, because I'm afraid he's out at the moment, but he'll be back at ten forty-five for a meeting with some clients.'

'The Earnshaws, I know. Look, the reason I rang was to let Dean know I can't make it. I've got to be somewhere else.'

'Certainly. I'll make sure he gets the message.'

'Good.'

He hung up, without even saying goodbye. How rude. Then she remembered her first day and the being "knocked into the planter" incident. He'd been incredibly rude then, too, and she hoped she wouldn't have much to do with Kristian Reynolds, if that was his attitude.

The phone rang again. 'Good morning, LandScape Ltd. How can I help?'

'What's your name?'

She narrowed her eyes as she recognised Kristian's voice. 'Esther.'

'Unusual.'

'Is it?' Her tone was sharp.

'I'm sorry, I'm not usually so…'

'Rude?' Esther supplied helpfully.

His chuckle took her by surprise. 'Rude,' he agreed. 'Please accept my apologies.'

This last was a little formal and stilted, and she guessed that he either wasn't used to saying sorry, or he didn't mean it but thought he'd better offer it.

'Accepted,' she replied.

'Good.'

Once again, he failed to end the call in the accepted manner and she was left holding a dead phone. She wasn't sure what to make of him. He was still bad-mannered and abrupt, despite the apology, but there had been that soft chuckle and his ready agreement that he was, in fact, rude. He could so easily have bawled her out for being inappropriate.

She wished Dean had filled her in a little more regarding his brother, but then he hadn't mentioned the other designer much, except to tell her his name and where to find his current client lists. She had no doubt that Kit's details could be found in one of the files, but knowing where he lived or what his national insurance number was wouldn't have prepared her for the reality of the man himself, and she still had the pleasure of meeting him in the flesh to look forward to. Although, she supposed that technically they already had met, if she counted being knocked backside-first into a planter as "meeting" someone.

At that moment, she heard a vehicle pull onto the drive and guessed it was probably Dean.

She was right. 'Kristian – Kris – phoned,' she told him as he strode into the reception area where her desk was located. 'He asked me to tell you that he's unable to make the meeting this morning with the Earnshaws.'

Dean rolled his eyes. 'Did he say why?'

'He has to be somewhere else.'

'That's all he said?'

'Yes, sorry.'

'He'll be the death of me,' Dean muttered darkly, shaking his head. 'Well, I don't suppose it can be helped,' he added in a more normal voice. 'I'll just have to make up an excuse as to why their designer can't be bothered to be here to discuss their garden and has left it to me.'

He saw her expression. 'Don't worry, I'm perfectly capable of talking them through it, but clients usually like to speak directly to the person behind the design. I'll get him to pop over before the weekend, to keep them sweet.'

'I've seen the projected cost,' she said. 'It is rather substantial.' She wondered what two and a half acres looked like. On paper it meant nothing to her, but from what she could tell from the potential costings and the detailed, glossy plans, the couple were having a maze, three Italiante terraces (whatever they were), fountains, statues, an orangery, and a willow arch, amongst other things.

'They've bought an old dilapidated manor house and are busy restoring it to its former glory, and that includes the gardens. From what I can gather, some parts of the house date from the seventeenth century. There are some before shots around somewhere...'

Dean glanced around helplessly, as if he expected them to materialise out of thin air right in front of him.

'Do you need them for the meeting?' she asked.

'No, it's OK.'

Esther made a scribbled note to find them and file them with the rest of the Earnshaw's documents. She'd already made significant inroads into the previously somewhat scattergun approach to filing, but there was only so much she could achieve in a week, especially since there was a great deal to learn and everything was so new.

'Was he…?' Dean floundered. 'How did he seem to you?'

What could she say? She could be honest and tell her boss what she really thought of his brother or she could be diplomatic. Diplomacy won.

'I'm not sure,' she said. 'I've only spoken to him a couple of times, so I don't feel I know him well enough to comment.'

He nodded slowly. 'I see,' he said, though what he "saw" was anyone's guess, as Esther was certain she'd given nothing away.

'He's… um, going through a bit of a bad patch at the moment,' her boss added, after a pause. 'I'm sorry he knocked you over. I did speak to him about it. When he called, did he apologise?'

She winced. 'Sort of.'

He let out a deep sigh. 'Sometimes I despair of him, I really do,' he muttered, as he wandered into his office.

She watched him go, then went to prepare a tea tray ready for the imminent arrival of his clients. It was while she was arranging some slices of apple and cinnamon cake on a plate, that the door opened. Expecting it to be the Earnshaws, Esther dashed out of the kitchen and into the reception area to be greeted by a delivery man holding a huge bouquet of flowers.

'Are you…?' he checked his hand-held device. 'The Girl Friday?' he asked.

Esther didn't know. Was she? She stared at him blankly.

'This *is* LandScape Ltd?' The delivery man glanced around.

'Yes.'

'Then I've got the right place. Here.' He thrust the bouquet at her, and she took it automatically, feeling rather bemused.

'Can you get me—?' Dean emerged from his office, then stopped and blinked at the sight of the flowers. 'An admirer?' he asked.

'They're not for me. At least, I don't think they are. They're for the Girl Friday,' she read, spying a little envelope on a plastic stick in the middle of the blooms.

Dean chuckled, sounding remarkably like his brother. 'Then they *are* for you.'

She stared at him. '*I'm* the Girl Friday?'

'Sorry.' He didn't sound it, she thought. 'I referred to you as that once, and it looks like it stuck. Well, not you specifically. All I said was that I needed a Girl Friday, and… well… you're it.'

'These are from you?' Even as she said it, she knew the flowers weren't from her boss, and she took a guess. 'They're from your brother, aren't they?'

'Probably. Check the card.'

Esther checked. There was one word typed on it. "Sorry".

She showed it to Dean, who shook his head. He seemed to do an awful lot of that where his brother was concerned.

'He's incorrigible,' he said.

She agreed with him. She also thought Dean's brother was arrogant and egotistical. Firstly, how was she supposed to know they were for her, and secondly, how was she supposed to know who they were from? But as she rooted around for a bucket or something to put them in – for a company whose sole purpose was all things gardeny, there was a severe lack of vases or buckets – she realised that she would have known, without Dean having to tell her.

Maybe Kristian Reynolds wasn't as incorrigible as she thought.

CHAPTER 27

Kit smiled and shook his head as he thought about the conversation he'd just had with LandScape's newest member of staff. He'd tried Dean's mobile first, but it had been switched off, so then he'd tried the landline, and had been momentarily surprised when a female voice had said, 'Good morning, LandScape Ltd. How can I help?' until he remembered their recently appointed PA.

'You're the new girl,' he'd blurted abruptly, just as he'd remembered that he'd inadvertently and unwittingly knocked the poor lass into one of the large planters beside the door, and he'd not even noticed. He'd meant to apologise, but life had got in the way, and he hadn't got around to it. It was probably too late, now—

He'd introduced himself and there'd been a bit of confusion about his name and then she'd thought he was one of LandScape's designers, which had made him roll his eyes. If she was Landscape's Girl Friday, he was the Man Friday. Both he and Dean did equal amounts of the designing, but it was Dean who smooched the clients and Kit who sorted out problems, chivvied along the contractors, and got his hands dirty. The arrangement suited them both.

She had sounded efficient and professional on the phone, and his first impression was that she was a good front-of-house person for the business. His second was that she seemed nice and, late or not, she still deserved an apology.

It was while he was ordering a bunch of flowers to be sent to her at work that he realised he didn't know her name when the florist, who'd assured him the bouquet would be delivered within the hour, had asked who they were for.

'Girl Friday,' he replied.

'And the message on the card?'

'Sorry.'

'That's all, nothing else?'

'No, just sorry.' What more was there to say?

Flowers ordered, he realised that he did need to know her name. It was rude and rather remiss of him not to know it, so he'd rung her back and she'd been just as sassy the second time as she'd been the first.

Dean was right; he'd not met her yet, but he liked

her already.

There was something odd though, and he was pretty sure it was a coincidence; the woman he'd driven home the other night, the woman whose handbag he'd returned, was called also Esther.

He couldn't fail to notice that the two bouquets he'd sent in the recent past, were both to women called Esther. How strange was that?

He hadn't realised that Esther was such a common name.

CHAPTER 28

When Giles hadn't contacted her by Thursday, Esther assumed he wasn't interested. Then out of the blue, he'd phoned her on Saturday morning and asked if she'd like to go out for a drink later that evening, suggesting a wine bar in town.

She'd debated whether to say yes or not, but what was the alternative? Sitting at home alone with a bag of crisps and crap TV for company. So she had agreed. There might not have been a spark last time, but he'd been pleasant enough and was good company, and she never knew, he might grow on her.

He was late. Esther hated being late herself and she wasn't too keen on other people being late either, so Giles's tardiness wasn't a particularly good start to the evening.

It went even more downhill when he crept up behind her just as she was staring at Flamingo Cam, which was now back to pointing at the bar. 'Hello, gorgeous!' he said loudly in her ear.

'Argg!' Esther jumped, and her knee caught the underside of the table and spilt the drink she'd bought so as not to look conspicuous. She scooted back, trying not to let any of the red wine drip onto her trendily-ripped pale blue jeans.

'Can I get you another?' he asked.

'You'd better,' was her rather cross reply. 'And ask for some paper towels to mop this up, please.'

'Coming right up!'

She was putting her phone away when he returned with their drinks.

'Why the frown?' he wanted to know.

She should have said, "because you're late and you made me spill my drink," but what actually came out of her mouth was, 'I've just watched my ex-boyfriend canoodling with another girl.' She took the paper towels from him and began mopping and wiping.

Josh was doing it on purpose, aware that she might be watching, and from the glee on his face, the bastard thought it was one big joke. Why on earth did she keep doing this to herself? She didn't really want to know what he was getting up to, and she wasn't all that anxious to catch a glimpse of the face she'd once loved, either.

Because "once" was the operative word. His

actions had killed anything she'd felt for him, but morbid curiosity had her reaching for her phone at idle moments.

The man on Cottage Cam wasn't to be seen (his house was empty this evening as far as she could tell), so she'd tuned into Josh and his outrageous antics. She'd noticed that she was too busy in her new job (which she loved) to keep clicking on the webcam, although she sometimes had a quick peek at Cottage Cam during her lunch break. The only time she tended to go online now, was when she was bored in the evenings. If she had something better to do, the thought didn't cross her mind. But this evening she'd been left waiting in a bar, tapping her toes and feeling like a right prat. No wonder she'd resorted to taking a sneaky peep at Flamingo Cam.

Esther realised Giles had fallen silent, but his eyes were roaming around the bar. 'What?' she asked, taking a sip of her fresh drink.

'Is he here?'

'Who?'

'Your ex?'

'Why would he be?'

'I don't want any trouble.'

'Eh?' Giles had lost her – she had no idea what he was talking about.

'You said you'd watched your ex making out with

another girl, so I assumed he is here, in this bar.' He was still scanning the room.

'He's in Spain. Malaga to be exact.' Esther said.

'I see. Don't you hate it when that happens.' Giles took a long swallow of his drink, pushing the straw to one side. She wondered what was in his glass. It looked like a cocktail of sorts.

'What? Malaga?' she asked, her confusion deepening. He wasn't making much sense at all, and she wondered if this was his first drink of the evening.

'When exes post stuff on Facebook and Instagram. It's as if they're trying to make you jealous.'

Ah, now she got it. 'He didn't post anything. I saw him on a webcam.'

Giles frowned. 'I'm sorry? A webcam?'

'Yes. Hang on.' She took her phone back out of her bag and brought up the relevant page. 'Look.' She turned the screen around for him to see.

'That's a bar or a nightclub,' Giles said, frowning.

'It's a bar called the Pink Flamingo, and that's my ex. He's doing it again. See?'

Giles saw and he clearly wasn't all that enthused.

'Sorry.' Esther immediately felt guilty. 'I shouldn't be showing you pictures of my ex,' she said, realising that she'd probably blown it with Giles. Oh well, never mind, she hadn't been into him all that much, anyway. Not at all actually, if she was honest.

'Is that live? Like, in real-time?' he asked.

'Yes. It's both cool and disturbing at the same time, don't you think?'

'How did you find it? I mean, did your ex email you the link, or something?'

'No, although I wouldn't have put it past him if he'd known about it. I found it by accident when I was Googling the bar and the webcam popped up. Anyone can see it.' She showed him, taking him back to Pink Flamingo's main site. 'This isn't the only one. There are loads of them out there.' She clicked on some of the others, to demonstrate. 'Look, you can see Paris, Rome, Barcelona, Scarborough…'

Suddenly Giles was doing a Sinead, his eyes roaming around the walls and ceiling. 'Do you think this place has a webcam?' he asked abruptly.

Esther realised he was looking decidedly nervous. 'I don't know, I haven't checked,' she said. 'But there is a camera on the high street which can be accessed by the public, and one down by the river, although that one mainly shows the swans and the occasional person throwing them some bread. Are you OK?' He'd gone very pale, she noticed.

'Erm... I'm sorry, but I have to go. I shouldn't have… Um… Er… Sorry.' And with that Giles was out of his chair, out of the bar and, she suspected, out of her life.

Go Esther, she said to herself, you really do know how to impress a guy.

CHAPTER 29

Monday was a glorious day. The sun shone out of an azure sky which had barely a cloud in it, the breeze was soft and warm, and the smell of summer hung heavily in the air. Along with a faint aroma of manure. She *was* out in the countryside, she supposed, so what did she expect?

Deciding she'd had enough of being cooped up indoors, Esther took her sandwiches out of the fridge in the little kitchen and popped them in her bag, deciding to explore the village during her lunchbreak.

LandScape Ltd was on the edge of Middlewick, so she strolled along the path for a few minutes until she came to the village green. Children were playing on the swings and seesaw, and there was a wooden climbing frame that looked like great fun if you were five years old. Benches were dotted around the outside of the play area and on the edge of the little duck pond, and she chose a bench away from the mums supervising their little ones, knowing that anxious parents needed to be able to sit close to the play area. She, on the other hand, would take great delight in throwing her crusts to the pond's feathered occupants.

There was a flurry of interest from the ducks and they paddled over as she plonked herself down on a bench and unwrapped her lunch. It was a BLT today, with a cupcake for after and a bottle of water to wash it all down. It mightn't be much, but it seemed like a feast to be able to eat it outside in such picturesque surroundings and on such a beautiful day.

She relished every mouthful, although she did shoot a few envious looks at the people sitting at the tables in the pub's garden, and even more envious looks at their drinks, the glasses sparkling as the sun caught the condensation on the outside. A chilled glass of cider would go down a treat on a day like today, but she never, ever broke her own rule about drinking at lunchtime on a work day. Besides, she wasn't all that keen on being in a pub by herself, and this had been reinforced by Giles's rapid departure on Saturday night.

She hadn't been surprised that she hadn't heard from him since. Fancy talking about an ex-boyfriend to a potential new boyfriend while on a date? Not only that, she'd more or less admitted to stalking him. No wonder the poor man had scarpered. If the shoe had been on the other foot, she might have run screaming for the hills, too. He must have thought she was a right nutcase.

After she'd finished eating, she decided to stretch her legs and go for a stroll, and Wildflower Lane drew her towards it. The name had caught her attention the first time she'd seen it when she'd been on her way for her interview, and she recalled a sea of brightly nodding flowers as she'd driven past.

There were even more blooms today she thought, as she turned into the lane and strolled along the rather narrow pavement. It was narrow because most of the available space either side of the tarmac was taken up with grassy verges and the pretty flowers they contained.

She wished she knew what they were. Bright purple, cream, fiery orange, zingy yellow, and every shade and colour in between danced and bobbed in the gentle breeze, and as she walked Esther ran her fingers gently through their waving stems, feeling the soft caress of petals on her skin.

The scent was amazing too, and she thought she recognised the smell and sight of one of the plants tumbling over a garden wall. The bright green leaves and delicate cream and pink blossoms were almost certainly honeysuckle, and she breathed in deeply, the fragrance reminding her of her parents' garden and the summers of her childhood.

It really was quite magical, she thought. It was incredible how a few simple flowers could be so effective. Not only that, the houses either side of the lane looked as if they should belong in an old-fashioned painting.

Chocolate-box, she thought the expression was. Most had thatched roofs, and she stopped outside a wrought iron gate to peer through it and admire the craftsmanship of the thatch. Not that she herself would want to live in a house with straw on the roof, but it did look incredibly pretty.

The butterscotch stone the cottages were built from, glowed in the sun, bringing to mind the house displayed on Cottage Cam, and she was even more convinced the property was somewhere in the UK, because it was so characteristically English.

Oh look, that one was incredibly pretty. The front garden had a small pond with bright orange flowers on tall stems growing along its edge. Was that a dragonfly hovering over the water? Yes, it was, she was certain of it, and birds flittered and fluttered in and out of the bushes, while the soft drone of bees provided a deeper note to the lively chirping.

No wonder there was so much wildlife here, what

with all the pollen and nectar that the thousands of flowers must produce.

The only thing that marred the perfect scene was a large black car on the drive. It seemed totally out of place in the idyllic, country cottage setting, but she supposed the owners had to park it somewhere. As she moved past the cottage's gate, she frowned.

The vehicle looked familiar… remarkably like the one she'd seen belting down LandScape's drive the day she'd ended up with her behind planted in a planter. Then she shrugged – she had no idea about cars, and one shiny black car was much like another.

The next house along was almost as pretty, with a red tiled roof and loads of tubs and hanging baskets. In fact, as she wandered up the lane, turning around when the cottages gave way to fields to stroll back down the other side into the heart of the village again, she was hard pressed to decide which house she liked the most.

They were all so very lovely and she envied those people who were lucky enough to call one of them home.

She did have a favourite, she realised as she dawdled past the one with the little pond in the garden, in spite of the large car marring its beauty. There was something about the place that spoke to her.

Ah well, enough daydreaming, it was time to get back to work. And if Dean was in his office, she'd ask him the names of some of those wildflowers.

CHAPTER 30

Esther switched on her laptop and as she waited for Cottage Cam to load, she delved into the fridge for the ingredients for dinner.

It was getting to be a habit, turning on Cottage Cam while she was cooking. Not that she "cooked" that often. For the first few weeks after Josh had left she hadn't felt the urge. Now that she was feeling more like herself, the weather had turned warmer and she'd been living on salads, with the odd pasta meal thrown in for good measure, so she still hadn't been doing much cooking.

But tonight Charlie, Sinead, and Abbie were coming to dinner and Esther intended to pull out all the stops. She planned Thai fish cakes for the starter, chicken in a creamy bacon, mushroom, and garlic sauce for the main course, and red berry pavlova for dessert, accompanied by several bottles of wine which were already chilling in the fridge.

She was delighted, and slightly spooked, to see Cottage Cam Man (she must think up a proper name for him) doing the same thing in his kitchen, and she watched as he opened a bottle of wine and placed it on the countertop to breathe. Esther didn't intend letting hers breathe – the wine would lose all its fizz. She had a feeling that his single bottle would have cost more than her four bottles put together.

She put the sautéed potatoes to one side, then decided to light a couple of candles. Not because it would be romantic, but because the glow was pretty and they infused the air with the gorgeous scent of vanilla and magnolia. And when she glanced back at the laptop screen, she noticed Cottage Cam Man was doing exactly the same thing.

Ooh, now that really *was* spooky. But it was comforting at the same time, as though she was actually sharing the experience of cooking dinner with someone. It almost felt as though the two of them were preparing food together, in the same kitchen.

Esther wondered what he was making. It was difficult to tell because of the angle of the camera, but she had a feeling the oven was involved because every so often he would bend over and disappear from view, and a faint cloud of steam would appear in his place. She had a hunch he was quite a good cook, although she had nothing to base this assumption on except for the fact that he seemed to know his way around a kitchen.

As for the woman Esther had caught a glimpse of a while back, she didn't think it was his wife. She'd come to the conclusion that he didn't have one, otherwise Esther would have seen her more often. Girlfriend, then? Possibly.

Knowing that the woman didn't live in the cottage with him, didn't make it any easier to accept the fact that he was taken, and that was that.

Eh? Esther paused – what on earth was she thinking? As if a girlfriend would make any difference since there was no chance of them ever meeting, and she had no idea where he lived or who he was. Cottage Cam Man aka... hmm. What would a good name be for him, she mused, as she bent down to her own oven to check on the progress of the chicken in its gently bubbling sauce. The smells permeating her little kitchen made her mouth water. She wasn't a particularly good cook, but she used to try her best to put a meal on the table every night. Josh always came home hungry, but even though he was frequently home before her, he had never cooked, always expecting her to do it.

It was nice to see a man who wasn't too lazy or too scared to use an oven, she decided, watching the man in the cottage stand in front of his kitchen window. A cloud of steam billowed up, and she guessed he might be draining hot water out of a pan. Ooh, she wished she could see what he was preparing.

The steam cleared and he turned away from the sink, giving her a good look at his profile. He definitely reminded her of someone, but who? He looked a bit like Chris Hemsworth when he didn't have any stubble. That was it, she'd call him Chris for want of anything better.

What had she been thinking before she'd been side-tracked? Oh, yes, she'd been debating the likelihood of ever meeting this guy.

Nil. Zero. Zilch.

That was the probability, so it didn't matter whether he was attached or not.

Dinner was nearly ready. As soon as the girls arrived, they could eat. They were due at any moment and just as she thought about it, Esther heard the buzzer sound and dashed into the little hallway to open the downstairs door.

She shot back into her own kitchen, desperately wanting to carry on watching the man on the screen, but the sound of footsteps on the stairs prompted her to hastily shut the lid of the laptop. It probably wouldn't do to let her friends see her like this. They thought she was beginning to move on, that her addiction to Flamingo Cam was becoming weaker as her love for Josh died. And that was true – she hardly bothered with Flamingo Cam anymore.

She'd replaced it with spying on Chris instead.

It seemed far more real than watching Josh sticking his tongue down a random girl's throat while swinging his hips to the music and trying to look cool.

Esther thought he looked a bit of a tit.

In fact, she'd got to the stage where she wasn't entirely sure what she'd seen in her ex in the first place.

Which was good. She was moving on.

But, darn it, she was lonely, and in the middle of the night when the sounds of the street outside were muted and the only thing to keep her company was the bright, shiny unreality of the internet, she longed for a warm, loving body to cuddle up to.

Damn you, Josh.

CHAPTER 31

Well, well, well, that was a surprise, Esther thought, as she dropped her phone back into her bag. She'd more or less given up on internet dating after Giles, and hadn't checked the site in several days, although she had ignored a couple of notification emails. Today though, she'd decided to get back on the proverbial horse. If romance wasn't going to come to her, then she'd have to jolly well go out and find it. And she wasn't going to do that by sitting at home night after night feeling sorry for herself and watching strangers on the other side of a camera. Whether they were on TV or a webcam, there wasn't any difference. She had to be proactive and not pathetically hope that a fella would conveniently land in her lap. So she'd taken a good long look at the dating site, had pinged off a couple of messages, and had just this very minute received a reply.

She had a date! Another one. *And* he seemed promising. Mind you, so had Giles, but she'd scared him off before she'd had a chance to decide whether she liked him or not. Maybe she'd have better luck with this one, which was why she vowed not to mention ex-boyfriends or webcams.

As she approached the wine bar where they'd agreed to meet, she ran through the few details she knew about him: his name was Robin, he was twenty-nine, worked in insurance in the city, liked fun nights out and romantic nights in, and was looking for a long-term relationship with the right girl. On paper, he sounded pretty good, and his photo had shown a fairly good-looking guy with dark hair, a wide smile, and twinkling eyes.

And there he was, looking exactly like his photo, which was a nice surprise. He was perched on a stool and lounging back against the counter, one leg cocked nonchalantly, his attention on the door, so he saw her as soon as she entered the bar. She hoped he liked what he was seeing, as he slipped off his stool and walked towards her, holding his hand out. She took it, and he pulled her in for a quick air kiss on the cheek.

Hmm, not bad, she thought – his greeting was neither too formal nor too familiar. He'd pitched it exactly right.

'Shall we find a table?' he suggested, and she

readily agreed, relieved to discover that she found him rather attractive and didn't feel the need to make an excuse to leave. Not yet anyway. Time would tell if this first impression was an accurate one.

Robin had a vodka and Esther asked for a gin, and when they had their drinks in front of them, they settled down to get to know each other a little.

They'd planned to meet at nine o'clock. Esther hadn't wanted to meet any earlier in case she couldn't take more than an hour or so of his company, but before she knew it, the time was ten-thirty and she was thoroughly enjoying herself.

He was funny, attentive and, more importantly, he seemed to be interested in her as a person, asking questions and actually listening to her answers, and she found herself regaling him with amusing anecdotes about the various places she'd worked and the odd things she'd been asked to do.

'I'm not temping anymore,' she said, realising she only had a small amount of wine left in her glass (was this her third or fourth drink? she couldn't remember). 'I'm now working as a PA for a landscape company and I love it.'

'Don't you miss the variety?' he asked.

She shook her head. 'I'd had enough of it. It used to be fun, meeting new people all the time, going to new places, but now I'm perfectly happy knowing I've got a desk of my own and I don't have the stress of learning where the loos are, or worrying that I'm stepping on someone's toes if I hang my coat on the wrong hook. Yes, that did really happen and the guy whose hook it was refused to speak to me for the whole time I was there. I like the familiarity of working in one place, and of not having to deal with a new set of office politics every couple of weeks, or constantly feeling like the new girl. And my boss, Dean, leaves me to my own devices most of the time. I've still got tonnes to learn about the business itself and I still can't tell a daisy from a dahlia, but I know how to run an office and that's what I'm good at.'

'I like a bit of variety,' he said. 'Doing the same thing day in, day out is boring.'

She tilted her head to one side and said with a smile, 'I didn't think insurance was particularly interesting.'

He grinned and a dimple appeared in each cheek. He really was rather attractive in a boy-next-door-meets-ruffian combo. She couldn't decide which one he was.

'It depends what's being insured,' he said. 'We don't do household insurance on your average two-up, two-down terraced house, and we certainly aren't interested in giving you a quote on your Ford Fiesta.'

'What do you insure?' she asked, knowing he was

teasing and quite liking it.

'Classic cars, luxury vehicles, the odd yacht.' He paused. 'We tend to have clients who come to us for their insurance needs, and we source it for them. I've been asked to sort out insurance for things like racehorses, a pianist's hands, an extremely ancient tree… the list is endless and rather varied.'

It sounded it, but she couldn't get away from the fact that insurance was insurance, no matter what. Still, if it floated his boat then who was she to argue? She'd never in a million years have thought she'd settle down in a small garden design company based in a little village out in the sticks. It just goes to show, she mused.

'Fancy another?' he asked, tilting his glass at her.

It was getting on a bit and she had work in the morning… oh, what the hell, another wouldn't hurt. 'Let me get these,' she offered, reaching for her purse.

'Definitely not.' He pushed his chair back and got to his feet.

'But you bought the others. It's my turn,' she insisted.

'When I take a girl out, I don't expect her to pay,' he said, and Esther felt a warm glow in her chest.

That was so sweet of him and so gallant. Even though she fully expected to pay her way, it was lovely to be treated like a lady. However, if they did end up going on another date, she'd have to insist on going half because it wasn't fair to expect the man to pay for everything. Besides, her pride wouldn't let that happen.

'OK,' she agreed, subsiding back into her seat. 'Another white wine, please.'

Robin, though, had other ideas and he returned with something pink and fizzy in a glass large enough to double as a goldfish bowl. Slices of fruit and cubes of ice floated on the top.

'That's not wine,' she observed.

He lifted an eyebrow and smiled. 'Clearly not. It's a cocktail.'

She could see that for herself and she wrinkled her nose at him. 'What's in it?'

'Try it, then I'll tell you.'

Esther angled the purple straw towards her mouth and took a sip. 'Mmm, that's yummy.'

'I thought you might like it. It's a bit too sweet for me, but girls seem to go for it. It's called a Cupid's Hope.'

Aww, how cute. 'Vodka?' she guessed, taking another sip. Quite a lot of vodka...

'Yeah, and pear juice and some other stuff.' He waved a hand airily, and she hoped the "other stuff" wasn't yet more alcohol. She'd be squiffy if she wasn't careful. The last time she'd drank too much she'd ended up booking a holiday that she didn't want to go on and couldn't afford, and she'd vowed never to get drunk again.

But it would be churlish not to drink this since he'd bought it for her. She wondered if he'd chosen it because of the name, and hoped he had. He might be a bit on the flash side, but she was beginning to suspect it might be a smoke screen hiding deeper more romantic feelings underneath. Cupid's Hope – she had the same hope, too.

Twenty minutes later, she was down to the last few sips in the bottom of the glass and the end of her nose was starting to feel a bit numb, a sure-fire indication that she'd better stop drinking right now if she didn't want to land herself in hangover hell come the morning.

She'd had a lovely evening, with a thoroughly nice man. He was definitely attracted to her, she thought, because he kept catching her eye and giving her long lingering looks. Smouldering, that's what they were. She wasn't quite doing any smouldering back, but she was certainly attracted to him. He was extremely good looking and she was flattered that he seemed to find her desirable. Not that she had any intention of doing anything about it tonight, but if he asked her out on another date she'd be more than happy to accept.

He helped her on with her jacket and opened the

door for her as they left the wine bar, and Esther's opinion of him ratcheted up another notch. She could get used to this, she thought.

'Can I give you a lift?' he asked, adding, 'Don't worry, I'm not a mad axe murderer or anything,' when she hesitated.

'OK,' she said, although the thought that she wasn't being wise flashed through her mind. Not only was she about to jump into a car with a strange man, if he took her home then he'd know where she lived.

Oh, for goodness sake, she said to herself. If he was planning anything untoward, it would have been far easier for him to slip something into her drink, than hope she'd agree to him giving her a lift home.

He took her arm and they walked slowly along the road until they reached his car, and she wasn't surprised to see that it was a low-slung sports model.

It took her a while and a bit of manoeuvring to get into the passenger seat, and she was glad she was wearing jeans and not a short skirt, but once she was inside, the leather seat curled around her like a lover's arms and she sank back into it. This was a first for her – she'd never ridden in a sports car before and she was slightly alarmed to discover how near she was to the ground.

'Your place or mine?' Robin asked.

'Pardon?'

'I said, your place or mine?'

'Er, mine.' She sent him a questioning glance.

'I hope there's somewhere safe to park this baby overnight,' he said, switching the engine on.

'Excuse me – overnight?'

'Yeah.' He smirked at her and licked his lips. 'I'm looking forward to seeing what you keep in those tight jeans of yours.'

Esther's mouth dropped open. 'Say that again?' She must have misheard him; she thought he'd said—

'The blouse is a good move. Not too tight or slutty. It leaves a bit to the imagination and I'm imagining an awful lot, I can tell you.'

'*What?*'

He sent her one of his smouldering looks, except to Esther, it suddenly seemed more predatory than smouldering.

'What's the address then? Hurry up, I haven't got all night. Oh, wait a minute, yes I have. Aaaall night,' he drawled, patting her knee.

His hand began to slide up her thigh and she slapped it away.

'I've got to be gone by seven-thirty, though,' he added.

'You're not staying the night,' she said emphatically. 'You're not even coming in for coffee. And don't think that coffee is a euphemism for something else, because it isn't. I hardly know you.'

'Look love, I bought you your drinks all night, and that cocktail wasn't cheap.'

For a moment Esther was speechless. How dare he? How bloody well dare he! Anger surged through her and she itched to slap that smirk off his face.

'I didn't ask for the cocktail,' she hissed, keeping a lid on her temper with difficulty. 'I asked for a glass of wine. And if you think I can be had for the price of a couple of drinks, then you're sadly mistaken.' She made a grab for the door handle, acutely aware that she was sitting in a strange man's car, late at night, and no one knew where she was or who she was with.

The relief when the door opened was enormous and bolstered her courage enough to say, 'Not only that, but I offered to buy my fair share. You're nothing but a creep,' she added as she fell out of the ridiculously low car and onto the pavement.

'And you're a tease,' he retorted. 'I thought you fancied me.'

'Not as much as you fancy yourself,' she shot back, clambering somewhat inelegantly to her feet and backing away.

She waited until he'd driven off before she flagged down a taxi, and as she got in it she vowed to never, ever try internet dating again. She'd either have to meet guys the old-fashioned way or cry off men altogether, because there was no way she was putting herself through anything like this again.

Dear God, she certainly could pick 'em!

CHAPTER 32

It was another glorious summer's day, and Esther was out for one of her lunchtime walks. She'd decided to stroll along Wildflower Lane and take a few snaps. She'd tried describing some of the flowers she'd seen to Dean, but hadn't made too good a job of it, so she was none the wiser as to what most of them were called although she had managed to identify a poppy.

She halted, noticing that she'd reached what she thought of as the prettiest cottage on the lane, and the sight of the gorgeous garden made her smile. Unfortunately, the large black car parked on the small drive spoilt the picture again and she narrowed her eyes at it. She still couldn't be certain, but she continued to have the nagging feeling that it was the same one whose owner had knocked her onto her behind.

Dean himself lived in one of their converted barns,

so it was quite feasible that his brother lived in the village too. Squinting in the midday sun, Esther peered up at the cottage, once again admiring the honey-coloured stone and the traditional roof. The climber growing around the open porch was in full bloom, heavy with flowers which were the most gorgeous shade of blue. The colour reminded her of bluebells (she was pleased she knew the name of those lovely spring flowers) and she could have sworn the scent of them was being carried to her on the breeze.

It was difficult to tell though, because there were so many other flowers both in the garden and on the lane, and any one of those could be wafting its sweet perfume in the air.

The dragonflies were still there, darting and swooping, their flight so swift it was hard to keep track of them, and there were butterflies everywhere she looked. It was all so colourful and cheerful, that she assumed the owner of the cottage must have a perpetual smile on his or her face.

What she wouldn't give to live in a place like this, she thought. Her little flat, with absolutely no outside space whatsoever, appeared dismal and dreary by comparison. There was no life, no colour, and not that much light what with the windows being rather on the small side.

The car intruded on her thoughts again and she studied it more closely. She'd only seen the back of it as it had shot up LandScape's drive, and the last time she'd seen this particular car at the cottage it had been parked facing her. But this time it was facing the other direction, and it bore a strong resemblance to Kit's car. She couldn't be entirely sure, but there was the location to consider and the fact that this was a garden to be proud of. Although, if she thought about it, this type of garden probably wasn't the sort that a garden designer would have. This one looked as though it had been left pretty much to its own devices; not so much planned but grown organically. It was the epitome of a cottage garden (once again she was pleased with her knowledge), and so characteristically English. Everything about it reminded her of long summer evenings, strawberries and cream, afternoon tea, lawn chairs, rope swings hanging from trees…

Then there was that car, gleaming menacingly at her, out of place with its shiny chrome, polished metal, and chunky tyres. The only car which wouldn't look out of place in this setting was one of those old classic ones, where the driver wore driving gloves and had a tartan blanket in the boot along with a wicker picnic basket. Whereas this particular monstrosity wouldn't look out of place on the space station.

With a loud hmph Esther gave herself a mental shake and walked back to work. She'd spent enough time daydreaming and she'd be late back if she didn't hurry. Thank God Dean was a decent enough boss and probably wouldn't even notice if her lunchbreak had run over by a few minutes. She didn't like taking advantage though, so if she was late (and she was), she'd make it up at the end of the day.

'Are you still there?' a male voice on the other end of the phone demanded, as Esther picked up what she hoped would be the final call of the day. If she'd had finished at her normal time, she wouldn't have been here to answer it.

'Clearly,' she retorted, recognising the voice.

'Do you speak to all the customers like that?'

'Most certainly not. I'm polite and friendly to every client.'

'Just not to me?'

'You're not a client.'

'You've got me sussed. It's Kit.'

'I know.'

'Did you get the flowers.'

'Yes, thank you. They were lovely.'

'Were? Have you killed them already?'

'No, I have not!' Esther felt quite indignant – she might not know their names, but she knew how to look after a bouquet of them. No one ever bought her flowers, so this bunch was rather precious and she'd changed the water every day. One or two (the roses) had withered, but she reckoned she'd have a few more days out of the rest of them.

'Keep your hair on, Friday, I was only teasing.'

'My name is Esther,' she retorted.

'I know.'

'Kit.' She took a breath, trying to control her irritation. This man was rather annoying. 'Was there something you wanted, or can I go home?'

'Go home, it can wait,' he said with a chuckle, and with that he ended the call, leaving Esther with a dead phone in her hand.

She wished he'd stop doing that she thought, before wondering what it was that he'd wanted and what it was that could wait.

It rang again.

'It's Kit,' he said.

She guessed as much. 'What can I do for you?'

'Is my brother there?'

'He's in his office.'

'Can you tell him to stop playing silly buggers and answer his phone?'

'You really expect me to say that to him?'

'Why not?'

'He's my boss.'

'So am I.'

'Nevertheless…'

'Please? He might listen to you.'

Esther sighed. 'He might, but then again he might fire me.' She did wonder why Kit felt the need to involve her, but she didn't feel she should ask. There was obviously something going on between the brothers but whatever it was, it wasn't any of her business.

'He won't.' She loved how Kit sounded so certain.

'I'll be sure to pass the message on,' she said, shaking her head slowly. The guy was insufferable.

'Thanks. Have a good evening, Friday.'

The phone went dead again. Someone ought to teach him phone etiquette, she thought as she grabbed her bag from her desk drawer and hurried to Dean's office.

She knocked tentatively, before pushing the door open and popping her head around it. Dean was sitting at his sloping drawing board, one pencil shoved behind his ear and another in his hand.

'I've got a message from your brother,' Esther said. 'He wants you to stop playing silly buggers – his words, not mine – and answer your phone.'

Dean looked up at her. 'If he rings again, tell him—' He broke off. 'It doesn't matter. You shouldn't be caught up in all this, and we certainly shouldn't be asking you to pass messages back and forth. It's childish, but then, that's my brother for you.'

Esther smiled, not knowing what to say. Kit certainly did come across as rather juvenile, a direct contrast to his staid and somewhat reserved brother. But if she was honest, she found it a refreshing change. Kit hadn't proved to be in the least bit predictable so far.

'I'll be off now,' she said, and Dean glanced at the clock on his wall. It had spades, rakes, forks and other assorted gardening items where the numerals should be.

'Is that the time? I hadn't realised it was so late.' He arched his back, to ease out the kinks, and rolled his shoulders. 'Why are you still here?'

It was nearly an hour past her usual finishing time and although she had only been twelve minutes late back from lunch, she'd wanted to complete the task she was working on before she left for the day.

'I was sorting out the invoicing for that job over in Powick and I didn't want to stop only to have to pick it up again in the morning.'

'He's right, you know, you are a Girl Friday.'

Esther rolled her eyes. 'He actually calls me Friday.'

Dean's lips twitched. 'Better than Wednesday, that creepy child in *The Adams Family*.'

She smiled. 'I like the name Sunday.'

'I like the name Esther.'

She froze. Was her boss coming onto her? Crikey, she hoped not. He was a lovely guy and a great employer, but there hadn't been one single spark between them when they first met, and there still wasn't on Esther's part. She liked Dean, she really liked him, but not in that way. Oh dear, this was going to complicate matters. Besides, she'd had her fill of the opposite sex for a while…

'I didn't mean it like that,' he added, seeing her expression. 'One of my school friends had a granny called Esther – a feisty old bird.'

'Are you calling me an old bird?' Esther teased, to show him she hadn't taken it the wrong way (although she had).

'No!'

'Feisty?'

'I don't know you well enough to comment, but I suspect you might be.' He paused. 'Don't take any crap from Kit. He might be going through a bit of a tough time at the moment, but it's no excuse to be obnoxious.'

Esther nodded, curiosity sweeping through her. 'I won't. I can give as good as I get.' She hoped he'd expand on what he'd just said, but when he didn't say anything further, she turned to leave.

'Before I go,' she said, 'Does Kit live in Middlewick?'

'Yes, he does.' Dean's attention was back on his drawing board, squinting at it.

'Does he live in Wildflower Lane?'

He looked up again. 'Yes, why do you ask?'

'I thought I saw his car parked in one of the driveways. The one with all the flowers in the garden.'

'Yep, that's his.' A shadow passed across his face. It was only there for a second, and Esther thought she might have imagined it.

'It's stunning, isn't it?' Dean continued. 'The garden is at its best in spring and summer, but Kit's planted it so that it looks good in the colder months. He's a bit passionate about wildlife, and he's the reason there are so many flowers on the verges along his lane. He's been spreading wildflower seeds and planting bulbs for years. Next year he—' Dean stopped, and there was that shadow again. He was silent for a moment, then pulled himself together. 'Best get back to work. These plans aren't going to draw themselves.'

'See you tomorrow,' she said, and all the way home she hoped she'd get to meet Kit soon. Not only did she want to know what the issue was between him and Dean, but he was also her boss. The two men ran the company together and it was only right and proper that she should meet him, sooner rather than later. Him knocking her into a planter didn't exactly count!

CHAPTER 33

What the hell was Nancy playing at?

Kit stared incredulously at yet another letter from her solicitor, which had been waiting for him on the mat when he'd arrived home that evening. Not only did she want half of everything he owned but it seemed she was applying for him to support her financially even after their marriage had been dissolved. Surely she couldn't do that, could she?

Shit, but this was a mess. Although he knew it was too late to call his lawyer, he checked the time anyway. Yep, the office closed a couple of hours ago. Legal advice would have to wait.

At a loose end and unable to stop thinking about the disaster that was now his life, Kit wandered into the living room. The light was fading rapidly, but he didn't bother to turn any lamps on – the gloom suited his mood perfectly.

He slumped into a chair, resting his head against the squashy cushion, the unexpected prick of tears behind his eyes making him blink, and he rubbed at them angrily, hating feeling so pathetic. Marriages ended all the time and he doubted if many of the subsequent divorces were friendly. Why should he expect his to be any different?

But, dammit, he never thought it would come to this, and a mixture of pity, anger, and sadness flowed through him. He didn't know whether to rage or weep. Shuffling in his seat, he sat forward with his head in his hands. Sadness was winning, but he wasn't sure who the tears were for – the acrimonious end of a dream, or his own self-pity. Both, probably.

Cross with himself, he rubbed angrily at his cheeks, dashing away the wetness. Crying wasn't going to get him anywhere – it just made him feel vulnerable and defenceless. He needed to stay strong and focused if he was going to make it through the next few days, weeks, months.

He couldn't believe the woman who'd once told him that he was the best thing to have happened to her and that she loved him with all her heart, was now trying to wring every penny she could out of him. He felt as though he'd never really known her. She'd turned into a stranger, and a fairly horrid one at that.

Slowly he got up and walked over to the French

doors and stood there, looking out onto his garden, anger coursing through him. Yes, he was angry with Nancy for doing this to him, to *them*, but more than that he was furious with himself for being in this position.

Abruptly, he slapped his hand against the glass and yelled his despair and frustration into the darkness.

It was over, his marriage was over. And, if he was honest with himself, all he wanted now was to sever every single tie between them and never set eyes on the woman again.

The love he'd once had for her was well and truly dead. Even his sudden burst of anger was dissipating. All that remained was an empty shell and the determination to rid the last vestiges of her from his life. And he vowed that he'd never again let anyone get close enough to inflict the kind of damage on him that Nancy had.

Never.

***

Everyone seemed to have had a holiday this year except me, Esther thought, as she read a text from Sinead. Apparently, she was on the Greek island of Paros for two whole weeks with her boyfriend Ben, and was currently sitting outside at a beachside cafe there. If Esther looked at the webcam, she'd see her.

Wonderful, Esther thought as she opened her laptop and navigated to a popular site which hosted most of the webcams she'd been looking at. It used to be bad enough seeing posts on Facebook and Snapchat. Now it was possible for your friends to rub your nose in it in real-time. Not that that was what Sinead was doing, and Esther was delighted that her friend had managed to get away. She was just envious, that was all. So many places to see, so many things to experience, and everyone else appeared to be doing exactly that while she was stuck at home. The summer might be a good one, but it couldn't compare to a summer abroad where there were loungers, umbrellas, and a sea that didn't give you goosebumps if you so much as dipped a toe in it.

The ancient computer finally chugged into life, the screen revealing a small horseshoe bay with a little jetty and several boats. The far side had a sweep of golden sand and a smattering of whitewashed buildings.

I can't see you she texted. **There are quite a few people sitting outside, which one are you?**

OMG!! You're online!! I'll stand up and wave

Esther could see her now, waving frantically.

It's mad – I'm logged on too, and I can see myself waving. Weird or what!!! Sinead messaged back

It certainly was. It was like looking at a mirror through a mirror. One day somebody was going to disappear up their own webcam, she thought chuckling.

She exchanged a few more texts with Sinead, then left her to enjoy her wine in peace while she went off to do something equally as exciting. Not.

There was nothing she wanted to watch on the TV, so she settled for scrolling through numerous Facebook posts of crafty ideas and pet cats, until she got bored. It was inevitable that her thoughts eventually turned to the webcam once more.

Feeling a bit like a peeping Tom, she had a quick look at the beach in Paros, but the table where Sinead had been sitting was now occupied by two elderly ladies, so she moved on to Madrid, Milan, and then the Trevi Fountain. Viewing crowds of people in these places didn't seem as personal as viewing a friend without them knowing, so she had no qualms about people-watching for a while.

Finally, she clicked on Cottage Cam. Spying on a man in his own home (and let's be honest here, she said to herself, that was essentially what she was doing) when he didn't have the faintest inkling he was being watched, was a whole different ball game to watching people in public places, even Sinead. And although she knew it was wrong and that she should stop immediately, she couldn't. For some reason, she felt as though she had a sort of connection to him, despite the fact that she had no idea who he was or where he lived. He could be a serial killer for all she knew. And there was the added issue of the fact that he didn't even know she existed. How you could feel a connection to someone who had no idea of your very existence was beyond her. Oh, wait, she'd felt the same way about Justin Timberlake when she was sixteen…

For a moment, she didn't notice him. Twilight was setting in and there were no lights on in the cottage, and she was about to click on something else, when a movement caught her attention.

Chris, aka Cottage Cam Man, was sitting in the dark, leaning forward with his head in his hands. The movement she'd noticed had been him rubbing his face. Then he slowly got up and walked over to the French doors and stood there, looking out onto his garden. His face was in shadow, but she realised from his body language that something was troubling him.

Without warning, he slapped his hand against the glass, the door vibrating at the assault, and his mouth opened in a silent scream. Actually, she guessed it probably wasn't silent, and for once she was thankful that there wasn't any sound on this thing. She wouldn't have been able to bear it if she could hear his anguish in addition to seeing it.

Feeling even more like a voyeur than ever, she hastily moved to another site, but nothing else held the same appeal, so she closed the laptop down and sat in the encroaching darkness of her own home.

Dear God, but she was so terribly and utterly lonely. She had friends of course, but they were all in relationships and she missed having someone of her own to snuggle up with and to share the trials and tribulations of her day. She also had her family, but she could hardly expect her mum to pop around to the flat every evening to keep her company, could she?

Restlessly her gaze wandered around the living room. It looked better with the lights off, less dismal. The whole flat could do with a lick of paint, but before Josh had dumped her they'd been reluctant to spend the money – her, because she thought they were trying to save to buy a place of their own; him, because he had obviously been planning on buying a one-way plane ticket and a whole new wardrobe. Now that the possibility of owning her own place had well and truly flown out of the window, she found she couldn't afford to spend money on paint. Besides, she honestly didn't feel like wasting her hard-earned wages on doing up her landlord's property.

The only bright thing in the entire place were the pretty cushions on her bed. In a fit of pique, she'd splashed out on three new ones after Josh left, simply because he hated scatter cushions and didn't see the point in them. And the flowers from Kit Reynolds, although they were starting to droop and fade, despite her claim to the contrary when she'd spoken to him earlier.

Wasn't it amazing, she mused, that it had taken for Josh to bugger off to Spain for her to receive flowers, because he'd never bought her so much as a single rose in all the time they were together. And in the space of a few weeks she'd been given two lovely bouquets, one from the taxi driver and the other from one of the men who owned the company she worked for.

That taxi driver had been nice, she thought. Not that she remembered him, but he'd been kind enough to return her bag and for that alone she was truly grateful. Then he'd gone and sent her flowers which had freaked her out a bit. But he'd not contacted her since and she suspected he wasn't a stalker – just a bloke who wanted to see her again. As a date this time, not as a customer. The fact that he hadn't hassled her made her realise that he'd probably been genuinely interested in her.

Ah ha! She'd been complaining that internet dating

wasn't working (too many creeps) and that she needed to meet a man in the old-fashioned way, and she'd gone and done exactly that without realising. The problem was though, that she had no idea about him. He could be old enough to be her dad, or have horrendous BO, or simply not be her type.

But she was never going to find out unless she called him. He might turn out to be a bit grim, but on the other hand, she might be wildly attracted to him and want to have his babies.

One thing she did know was that he was kind and thoughtful.

She could do worse as a starting point.

On impulse, she had a quick look in the drawer where she'd thought she'd dropped his card into after the flowers had died, and found it straight away. Before her courage deserted her, she dialled his number and waited, worrying slightly that she was doing the right thing.

On the third ring, she ended the call, her heart thumping. Dear God, what was she doing? Had her life seriously come to this – phoning a man she couldn't remember just to alleviate the crushing loneliness? Thank goodness he hadn't answered.

***

When Kit finally walked back into his living room, he saw a number of missed calls. He'd been sitting in the little summer house at the end of the garden for hours, preferring to be alone with his misery, and had left his phone in the house, not wanting to speak to anyone in case he broke down in tears.

One call was from Dean, one from his mother, and another from a client, although why these particular people felt it was OK to speak to him outside of normal working hours was beyond him. It wasn't the first time that this particular client had called him in the middle of the night to check on a trivial detail, so he was relieved that he'd missed the call. He honestly didn't need to discuss the pros and cons of different kinds of coping stones at eleven o'clock at night. Some clients were an absolute pleasure to work with, but some were of the opinion that once they had commissioned you to do a job for them, they subsequently owned you.

He didn't want to call his mother back and risk her maternal radar sniffing out that something was wrong. Besides, it was too late and she'd probably be in bed. Dean had left a voicemail which he listened to and would action in the morning. The clients could also wait until then, too. However, there was a number he didn't recognise, and he stared at it for a while, trying to figure out who's it might be.

Meh, it was probably a sales call, he decided, or someone wanting to know if he'd been involved in an accident that wasn't his fault in the last three years. He should have answered – he could have told them about his car crash of a marriage, the ending of which definitely wasn't his fault…

He looked at the number again, wondering if he should call it to see what they wanted, before deciding that if it was important, whoever it was would have left a message, or would ring back.

And with that, he switched off his phone and headed for the fridge. He could seriously do with a beer or two, because he had a feeling it would be quite some time before he would be able to sleep.

CHAPTER 34

Esther hated mess and when she'd started at LandScape Ltd the files, both electronic and paper, had been all over the place. She'd made good inroads into them, starting with the most recent, figuring these would be the ones Dean and the others were working on now, and were therefore the most important, and working her way back.

During her rooting around, she'd come across loads of interesting things, and today she was digging around in one of the oldest filing cabinets where all the company's start-up documents were kept. They were a bit of a jumble, so she took all the folders and loose papers out, one drawer at a time, and tried to make sense of them and put them into some kind of order.

The company had been going for around eight years, she read, but there was stuff in these drawers which went back even further.

Ooh, look, there was a photo of Dean standing proudly in front of a garden which was all straight lines of concrete and steel, with some architectural planting (she was delighted that she knew what that was, because a few weeks' ago, she wouldn't have had a clue). He looked so young, and she chuckled at his longer hair and the earnest expression on his face. Reading the caption, she smiled. He'd won a competition to design a garden for one of the big electronic firms on the outskirts of Worcester, and this was the result.

There were a few more photos of the company's earlier work, and she scanned through some of the ones Kit had designed. Now that she thought about it and the evidence was right in front of her eyes, she could tell which garden was designed by which of the brothers without being told. They had quite distinctive styles, and she wondered if they ever collaborated.

Ah, yes, they did…

She unearthed a photo of the pair of them posing with the owner of a large house not far from here, where the brothers had designed and installed a modern take on an old-fashioned ornamental garden.

So, this was Kristian Reynolds, was it, she mused, holding the photo up to her face and squinting at it. It was about time she knew what he looked like. One of the reasons was because she didn't want to embarrass herself were he to walk through the door, and the other was sheer unadulterated curiosity. Dean was quite good-looking (it was a pity there was no spark between them, not even a glowing ember), so she had been wondering if Kit would be as easy on the eye.

Bloody hell, but he looked familiar! There was a certain family resemblance to Dean, but Kit was far better looking. And he really did remind her of someone. Someone she'd seen quite recently too, and she racked her brains to—

Oh! OMG!!!

Esther closed her eyes for a moment. No, surely not… it couldn't be…

She opened them again. It *was*, she was certain of it.

How was that for a coincidence? Her Cottage Cam Man, who she'd christened Chris (oh, the irony) was none other than Kristian Reynolds. Kit.

She'd stake her life on it that she was right.

It was definitely him. *Wasn't it?*

Esther began to doubt herself. As far as coincidences went, this one was a corker. And she, for one, didn't for a second believe that the man she'd been so avidly ogling through the safety of a camera lens was the same man who was one of her employers. Nah, it couldn't be him. But there might be a way to check and put her mind at rest.

Although she was fully aware that Dean wasn't in his office, she knocked anyway. It was a habit she'd started from day one and she wasn't about to break it, in case he'd sneaked back in when she'd had her back turned.

She popped her head around the door. The office was empty.

Good.

Esther closed it softly behind her, and knocked on the other office door – the one she'd rarely ventured into until now because it hadn't been used in the month or so since she'd been working for LandScape Ltd. As Dean had explained, his brother preferred to work from home or out in the field (so to speak), and rarely used his office.

Unlike Dean's obsessive neatness, this room gave the impression its owner had been interrupted whilst in the middle of a major project and would be back any second. It had been like this since her first day, although she had noticed the occasional file having changed position. However, she couldn't be entirely sure whether it was Dean who was responsible for moving stuff around, or whether it was Kit himself, coming to the office when she wasn't there.

Feeling like a burglar, Esther slid one of the desk

drawers open and rifled through it.

There was nothing with Kit's photo on. And the same was true for the next drawer, and the next. The final drawer, however, held what she was searching for.

Gingerly, she slid the photocopy of Kit's passport out from underneath a pile of papers and stared at it.

The man whose image stared back at her was the same man who she'd been watching on Cottage Cam.

Oh, dear. She swallowed convulsively She'd only been inadvertently spying on one of her employers…

But she realised to her consternation that she didn't regret one single look.

She also realised that her wish to meet Cottage Cam Man was definitely going to come true, sooner or later.

There was something else though, that concerned her far more, and that was the question of why there was a camera pointing directly at the rear of Kit Reynold's house, and, more importantly, *should she tell him*?

CHAPTER 35

Several hours later, and Esther still didn't believe what she'd discovered, despite the evidence. Throughout the remainder of the day, she kept clicking onto Cottage Cam to examine the back of the house. It certainly was in keeping with the front, *if* in fact Kit's house on Wildflower Lane was the same cottage as on the webcam. She couldn't see all that much of the garden itself, except for a small crazy-paved patio area with a table and a couple of chairs on it, but there were loads of plant pots (if you could call an old Wellington boot a plant pot) filled with flowers, and she was sure she could see butterflies and other insects busily flitting about.

Now that she came to think about it, the cottage on her screen was constructed from the same colour stone as the one on Wildflower Lane, and the thatch appeared very similar. Although she had to admit that it could be entirely possible that all thatched roofs looked the same – she was hardly an expert. However, if someone had shoved this image under her nose and told her it was the back of Kit's cottage, she probably would have believed them.

Now though, she wasn't sure what to believe, and her eyes and her imagination could well be playing tricks on her. So once again, the only way to know for sure was to see for herself. Which meant picking a time when she knew Kit wouldn't be at home.

She could hardly go snooping around his house when she was supposed to be in work, so that left the evenings or one day at the weekend. But she didn't know if she could wait that long – curiosity was already driving her mad. She simply had to know, one way or the other.

There was one thing that both Dean and Kit were meticulous about and that was keeping their electronic diary up to date. They shared the same one, with Kit's appointments in red and Dean's in yellow, so everyone could tell at a glance who was meant to be where.

Their hours weren't strictly nine to five either, although Esther's was. Both of the owners visited clients in the evenings, and her heart soared when she realised that Kit had just such a meeting the following evening at six-thirty, on the other side of Worcester. If she brought a change of clothes and a pair of flat shoes, she would be able to go sneaking around to her heart's content. Or for an hour or so, anyway. If she assumed he was working from home in the afternoon, he'd have to leave by six o'clock at the very latest (more like five-thirty, but she was erring on the side of caution here). If the appointment took an hour, plus another half an hour for the drive back, then he wouldn't be back until eight p.m. She had plenty of time.

Feeling naughty and spy-like, she spent some of the afternoon checking Google maps to see if there was an easy way to get around the back of Kit's house.

There wasn't, she discovered. Behind the prettiest cottage on Wildflower Lane was nothing but fields, and although she guessed there were probably footpaths and rights of way through them, she had no idea where to start. Therefore, she'd have to risk walking up his drive.

Which was the reason why she was feeling sick with nerves at six-thirty the following evening. The sun wasn't due to set for ages yet, so she didn't even have the cover of darkness to conceal her more-than-dodgy activities. What on earth could she say if one of his neighbours challenged her? She wished she'd thought to bring a file, then at least she could pretend she was bringing him something to sign. She didn't think she looked like a burglar, but then again she had no real idea what a genuine burglar looked like. They were hardly going to wear striped T-shirts and carry a bag with SWAG written on it, were they? For all his neighbours knew, she could be casing the joint.

It wasn't too late to back out. She could walk away now, and no one would be any the wiser. But that was the problem – neither would she. And her curiosity was driving her to distraction. She'd had trouble falling sleep last night for thinking about it, vacillating between feeling the truth of it deep in her heart, and telling herself she was being ridiculous. And yes, she had spent an inordinate amount of time watching the webcam, to no avail. The cottage had been empty and dark every time she checked on it until she'd eventually dropped off to sleep. It was also the first thing she'd looked at when she'd opened her eyes. And she'd taken every opportunity to glance at it throughout the day, too.

Once or twice she'd caught a glimpse of

movement, and the curtains had been drawn at some point and then opened again, but she'd not seen *him.*

She hoped she wouldn't see him now, either. Now would not be a good time to bump into Cottage Cam Man, not when she was trying to saunter down his drive and not look suspicious. She suspected she was doing a pretty poor job, but no one appeared from either of the houses next door to challenge her, and as she slipped into the shadow of the side of the house, she guessed she'd got away with it.

A little path led from the drive to a gate, the archway above it draped with fragrant climbing flowers. This was it. It was now or never. Once she'd opened the gate and stepped through it, there was no going back.

Her hand on the latch, she pushed it down, half expecting the gate to be bolted from the other side, but it opened when she gently pushed it and she slipped inside.

Oh, my, but the garden was so lovely it took her breath away.

If she'd thought the front garden was spectacular, this one was simply wonderful. Immediately outside the French doors was a crazy paved patio area, with a little table and a couple of chairs on it (like the garden in Cottage Cam, she realised, her heart thumping), and a little path meandered its way through beds jam-packed with flowers, towards a white picket fence with a small gate set into it. There were trees and tall shrubs either side of the garden shielding it from its neighbours, making it almost totally private, and beyond the gate Esther could see a meadow surrounded by hedgerows, and woodland in the distance.

Unable to resist, because the path drew her feet along it, Esther strolled dreamily down the garden. Ooh, look, hidden in the corner she caught a glimpse of a tiny summerhouse, painted the most wonderful shade of lavender. It was only visible now, because the early evening sun was shining directly on it. What a glorious place to sit and enjoy a glass of something tall and cold.

And there was another pond, larger than the one in the front, and was that a real live frog perched on a rock in the middle? Yes, she thought it was. As she examined the garden further she saw nesting boxes fastened to the tops of the tree trunks, and odd little structures filled with holes which bumblebees were entering and leaving in droves. Butterflies danced in a cloud around her head when she disturbed them as she trailed her hands along the flowers, and she laughed at the sheer beauty of their multi-coloured wings.

There was even a cute post-box, with roses growing wantonly around it and up it, and a hammock hanging between two of the larger trees, the invitation to gently swing and sway in its comfortable depths hard to withstand. She'd love nothing better than to sink into it and let the hum and buzz of the bees lull her to sleep.

This garden could so very easily be twee or corny, but it wasn't. It was, however, quaint and beautiful, and so very English country garden that it lifted her spirits and made her heart sing. Gardening had never been her thing having never had one herself, although she had seen the attraction of being able to sit outside in a lovely space and enjoy the outdoors, but today, in this magical place, she got it. She understood. She could stay here forever and never become tired of it, guessing that the gardener who was responsible for such a gorgeous garden would make sure that it would be as beautiful in autumn, winter, and spring. She hoped she'd still be able to view it then, because she longed to see how it changed with the seasons.

Ah. That was the reason why she was here in the first place, to discover whether this was

Cottage Cam or not, and whether the man she'd been watching was Kit Reynolds all along. For a moment or two, the garden had seduced her so completely that she'd forgotten the reason she was in it.

Taking a last lingering look at the meadow beyond the little picket fence, which was also filled with colour, the long grasses and flowers waving gently in the breeze and reminding her of lazy waves on a jewel-coloured sea, she slowly turned to take a proper look at the back of the cottage. She knew deep down that this definitely was Cottage Cam, but it wouldn't hurt to make sure.

Her heart stopped. *It was.*

Esther was staring at the very same floor-to-ceiling double doors that she'd been peering through for the last few weeks. There was the same view into the kitchen, although the angle was different and the cottage appeared further away as she stood at the end of the path by the gate, than it did when viewing it through a screen.

Wondering where the camera was, she tilted her head back and peered into the trees, narrowing her eyes against the slanting rays of the sun.

Could it be up there? No, she didn't think so, it wasn't quite right. Maybe—?

Without warning a loud masculine voice broke

into the lazy late evening calm, making her jump, and she realised she'd been caught red-handed.

'Who the hell are you and what are you doing in my garden?' it demanded, and she slowly turned to face Cottage Cam Man, aka Chris, aka her boss, Kit.

Oh, dear…

CHAPTER 36

Kit wasn't in the best of moods; his darned car had conked out on him. Not so much conked, rather it had told him he'd better not drive it any further as a warning light had shown up on the dash, and when he'd checked the manual in the glove box, it had informed him that he should cease driving the car immediately and take it to a garage without delay.

This involved calling the garage, waiting for a tow, and then getting a lift back home. He hoped to God it was nothing serious, but that was the problem, he couldn't tell and neither could the guy who'd driven the tow-truck. A diagnosis would have to wait until they could plug the car into the garage's computer. From the research he'd done while he was waiting, it could be anything from a faulty switch, to the engine in danger of blowing up at any minute.

The driver of the tow-truck had kindly driven him

home after dropping his car off at the garage, and he'd hopped out at the end of the lane rather than make the poor bloke do a U-turn in such a narrow road. Which was probably why the woman who was skulking in his garden hadn't been alerted to his arrival by the sound of an engine, and had jumped a mile when he'd demanded to know what she was doing.

With his hands on his hips, he was about to yell some more, when he recognised the girl who was standing halfway down his path, the sun illuminating her like some kind of angel. Or should he say fairy? Because she looked like a fairy princess in her fairy grotto.

For a second, he was speechless, then he cried, 'You!'

It was Esther, the girl he'd given a lift home to. The girl whose bag he had returned, had sent flowers to, and whom he hadn't heard from again. Until now.

Which begged the question, what was she doing in his garden? While he was at it, he'd also like to know how she'd found out where he lived. He'd only given her his phone number; he'd not even put his name on the card that had accompanied the flowers.

'I know and I'm sorry,' she said. She looked as though she was about to cry. 'I can explain.'

He put his hands on his hips. This had better be

good. He could think of no logical reason why this woman should be trespassing in his garden. She could hardly claim she was looking for her ball, could she?

She took a step or two closer and he eyed her cautiously. She was as pretty as he remembered, with her curling hair escaping from her bun and a smattering of freckles on her nose. She looked fresh and natural – completely different to Nancy's polished beauty. Nancy used to spend a considerable amount of time primping and preening. Kit had the feeling that Esther's prettiness was totally natural and that she needed to put very little effort into her appearance to look gorgeous. It was rather refreshing. Was that part of the reason why he hadn't been able to get her out of his head since he'd dropped her off at her flat that night?

'Go on then,' he urged. 'Explain.'

'There's a camera pointed at the back of your house.'

Kit felt his eyebrows rise to his hairline. 'Pardon?'

'There is, honestly.' She paused and glanced into the tree to her left. Kit's gaze followed.

'So?' He knew he was being belligerent, but if what she said was true, then how did she know about it when he didn't? Had she put it there? He narrowed his eyes, trying to see through the gently moving leaves.

‘Anyone can click on it,’ she said.

‘I don’t understand.’ Kit was utterly flummoxed.

‘Look.’ She took her phone slowly out of her pocket, as though he might have thought it was some kind of weapon, and when he made no move, her thumbs flew across the screen. ‘Can I show you?’

‘I think you’d better had,’ he advised. This situation was becoming weirder by the second.

She walked towards him, and when she drew close enough, she turned the screen around to face him.

Kit’s mouth dropped open.

He was looking at his own back garden, with his own self standing in it, Esther holding her phone out to him. He watched as she glanced behind her, seeing her screen self and her real self mirroring each other, and he thought that this was positively the most surreal experience of his life.

‘Where is it?’ he asked, trying to work out where the camera was located from the angle. It was definitely higher than the fence, because it was looking down on the scene, rather than up or straight across. He stared at the trees again but couldn’t see anything.

‘Over there,’ she said, pointing in the general direction of the rear of the garden. Her reply wasn’t much use, as he’d already worked that out for himself.

‘Did you put it up?’ he demanded.

'*Me?* No!'

'If you didn't, who did?'

'I've no idea.'

'How do you know about it?' he asked, feeling extremely unsettled to think that someone had been watching his every move. A horrible thought occurred to him. 'Did Nancy put you up to it?'

'Who is Nancy?'

He studied the woman closely, but as far as he could see, she was telling the truth. He still wasn't sure what to make of her, though.

'Never mind,' he said. 'How do you know about it?' he repeated,

She blushed. 'I was looking at another webcam – there are loads of them online, all the major cities and lots of other places – when I happened to click on this one. At first, I thought it was a film set or something, but I pretty quickly realised it wasn't.'

'But I still don't understand how you knew this was *my* house?'

'I didn't, not at first. It could have been anywhere, although I did think it was somewhere in England.'

'Go on.' He couldn't take his eyes off the screen and the two figures on it.

'I walk down this lane quite often on my lunchbreak because it's so pretty but I didn't make the connection until I was doing some filing and came across an old photo of you and Dean. When I saw it, I was pretty sure that you and the man I'd seen on the webcam were one and the same, but I wanted to be certain before I said anything.'

'You're Dean's Esther!' Bloody hell! He'd wake up in a minute and find he'd dreamt the whole thing.

She hesitated. 'I thought you knew who I was. You said, "you", as if you knew me?'

'Never mind,' he said again. She clearly didn't recognise him from that night, and he was too interested and concerned about this hidden camera to take the time to explain.

'I'm *your* Esther, too,' she said. 'I work for the both of you. Nice to meet you.' She stuck out her hand but withdrew it again just as quickly.

'You, too,' he replied absently. He'd tell her some other time that they'd already met. He was finding it difficult to get his head around the additional piece of information that his Esther was also Landscape's Esther. Maybe the name hadn't been as common as he'd thought?

'So you decided to break into my garden, rather than pick up the phone and call me?'

'I didn't break in!' she objected. 'The gate was unlocked.'

'You're still trespassing—'

'If that's all the thanks I get for letting you know

that everyone in the world with a smartphone can see you washing your smalls, then I wish I hadn't bothered.'

'Washing my what?'

'Smalls.'

'You haven't watched me washing my boxers,' Kit stated emphatically. She was making it up.

'Washing the dishes, then,' she amended Her blush deepened.

'Just how long have you been spying on me?' he wanted to know.

'Not long,' she said, but her voice was so quiet he could hardly hear her, and she couldn't meet his gaze.

He felt quite peculiar to think that this woman had been watching him while he was going about his everyday business, and he wondered who else had been watching.

'Right,' he stated, decisively. 'Let's see if we can find this camera, shall we?'

'You want me to help?'

'I think you owe it to me,' he said.

She frowned at him, the line which appeared in the middle of her brow making him smile. Even when she was cross, she was cute.

'I came here to tell you about the camera,' she said. 'I don't think I owe you anything else.'

'You didn't come here to tell me anything – I

caught you prowling around my garden.'

'I would have told you,' she said.

'When?'

'Eventually.'

He tilted his head and stared at her.

'It's not easy, you know, telling someone that there's a camera pointing into their house.'

'I doubt it is,' he said dryly. 'Let me get my phone out and find the link, then maybe we can use our screens to triangulate the camera's location.'

'Good idea. If one of us goes out of shot, then we know we've gone past it.'

But after scouring the garden, Kit was forced to come to the conclusion that the camera wasn't on his property at all. Together they stood by the gate in the picket fence and stared into the meadow.

'It's beautiful,' Esther breathed. And Kit had to agree, but he wasn't looking at the waving grass and the thousands of flowers dotted amongst the stems – he was looking at Esther.

The fading evening light caught the russet highlights in her hair and cast a faint pink glow across her face. Her eyes were alight with wonder and her lips were slightly parted. For one mad moment, he wondered what it would be like to kiss them.

He cleared his throat, trying to drive the disturbing thought out of his mind. What on earth was he playing at, imagining kissing this woman who he hardly knew and, more to the point, was technically an employee of his?

He tore his gaze away from her and focused on the landscape in front of him. When his attention was caught by the shelter, he gave it closer consideration, before dismissing it. Nah, he decided, the structure was too low. He could hardly see it from his garden, and only then if he was standing near the fence. Besides, the angle wasn't right.

He checked his phone.

Or was it?

'Esther, do me a favour and look towards that building there.'

'What is it?'

'It's not a stable, exactly. Rather, it's a shelter for the horses that used to be in this field.' He studied his phone. 'You're looking right at it. Look up a bit. A bit more. There. You're staring directly into the lens of the camera.'

'Yes,' she said. 'I most certainly am.' She pointed to a tall pole protruding from the top of the structure. There was a small black thing right at the top of it. 'I think we've found your spy.'

Kit burst out laughing. Oh, dear God. To think he'd stared at this scene a thousand times and never noticed a damned camera perched on the top of a pole. He'd never actually noticed the pole, if he was honest. He'd always been too busy looking at the flowers.

'How long do you think it's been there?' Esther asked. She was still looking rather serious.

'God knows! There used to be some valuable mares in this field. I suspect Amos Brinkman who owns them, installed the camera for security purposes. How it came to be pointing directly at my house, I've no idea. And as for streaming the feed to the world at large…' He shrugged.

'Why are you so amused?' Esther asked. 'I'd be horrified.'

'I'm happy because the mystery has been solved, and relieved that it's nothing sinister.' And, more significantly, it had brought Esther to him.

He would have met her eventually of course, but he felt a kind of bond with her which had nothing to do with the fact that she worked at LandScape Ltd. Was it something to do with that night when she'd jumped into his car, eyes wide like a frightened rabbit, demanding him take her home? He'd been unable to get her out of his mind ever since.

Ah, but the problem was she worked for LandScape Ltd. She worked for *him*. Was it ethical to date his staff? And, after Nancy, did he want to date anyone anyway?

Even if he did decide that a date with an employee was OK, there was the fact that he was still tied to Nancy to consider. He was in no fit state emotionally or financially to put himself out there again.

Besides, Esther hadn't called him after he'd sent her flowers, so she obviously wasn't interested in him. She probably had a boyfriend or a significant other, or she simply didn't fancy him.

He should walk away now, he decided.

Which was why he was quite taken aback when he found himself asking, 'Do you fancy going out for a meal sometime?'

And was even more taken aback when she readily agreed.

Oh, Lordy, he had no idea what he was doing, but it felt incredibly good.

CHAPTER 37

Despite passing the Willow and Wicket every day, Esther had never been inside the pub, and was delighted to see that it was pleasantly old-fashioned, with a gleaming dark wood bar, flagstone floor, an unlit wood burner at the far end, and a dog sprawled across its owner's feet as the man enjoyed a pint and read his newspaper.

Kit had informed her that they did lovely food, so she'd agreed to meet him in there for lunch the following day. When he'd suggested a meal she'd assumed he'd meant right there and then, but he'd mentioned lunch, which was a far better option because she could always use the excuse of needing to get back to work in case things became awkward.

Things were awkward enough already as far as she was concerned. Her employer had asked her out for a meal and she wasn't sure whether he thought it was a date or whether he was simply being friendly. She hoped it was the latter, because she was fairly sure he had a girlfriend, remembering the woman who she'd seen in his living room. But then, maybe they'd broken up and that was the reason why he'd been so upset a few days later. If he *was* free, then maybe this was a date after all. Or maybe this wasn't, and she was reading far too much into his offer of lunch. Oh, dear, had she said anything which had made her look a fool? Other than trespassing on his property and confessing that she'd been secretly ogling him online, that is?

She thought back.

No, she was safe. All she'd done was say, 'Yes, that would be lovely.' He could hardly read anything into that.

The one thing she had done when she'd arrived home last night, was to check the webcam. She'd been expecting it, but was nevertheless intensely disappointed to discover it was no longer available. When she'd tried the link, her screen informed her that the page couldn't be found. She'd been so used to checking in on him that she felt strangely bereft. But was it Cottage Cam that she was missing (and the man who lived there), or was she just addicted to viewing other people through a lens?

She'd clicked onto the Flamingo Bar instead, just

to check.

She hadn't looked at it since…? Actually, she couldn't remember the last time, and she also couldn't remember the last time she'd thought about Josh.

Josh, *who?* she giggled to herself, pleased to find that she was well and truly over her ex and managing perfectly well on her own. She was being frugal with her money, and with LandScape Ltd paying more than the agency had, she was even managing to save a little. She was a long way from being able to put a deposit down on a home of her own, but it was a start. Not working in the city centre helped too, as she wasn't tempted to go shopping in her lunchbreak and buy stuff she didn't need just to feel a momentary flash of fulfilment.

Looking back, had she been trying to compensate for the lack of happiness in her relationship by buying things? Maybe she had. Now that the shock of Josh's abandonment had faded, she was able to see their relationship much more clearly, and it hadn't been as wonderful as she'd thought. She'd been fooling herself by focusing more on the next steps of marriage and children, than on the man she would be taking those steps with. Come to think of it, he'd done her a favour by dumping her.

She felt as though she could genuinely move on now and forget about him.

But was moving on with Kit Reynolds (if indeed that was what this lunch was about) such a good idea?

It was too late now, though. She was already in the pub and so was he she saw, sitting at a table by the window. He stood to greet her and she half-expected a kiss on the cheek or a hug, but all he did was indicate that she should take a seat then ask her what she wanted to drink.

'I'll bring a couple of menus over,' he said, and she watched him walk over to the bar.

It was much better seeing him in real life than it was observing him on screen, she mused, not for the first time since he'd confronted her yesterday evening in his garden. He was taller than she'd expected him to be, and broader across the shoulders. Although she was trying not to be too obvious about it, she couldn't help noticing his muscular arms, with their smattering of dark hairs showing below his rolled-up sleeves. He had a flat stomach, too – she loved a flat stomach. And a nice bum, she saw, as he leant against the bar, waiting for their drinks to be poured. It must be all that outdoor work, she guessed. All that digging and raking, and hefting wheelbarrows full of earth.

Quickly she dropped her gaze as he turned around and began walking towards her, and she hoped he hadn't spotted her ogling him. She only looked up again when he deposited their drinks on the table and handed her a menu.

'I really must thank you properly for bringing the CCTV camera to my attention,' Kit said, taking a mouthful of his sparkling water. 'Amos, the farmer who owns the field and the horses, was mortified. He'd forgotten all about the camera and hadn't looked at it in weeks. He disconnected it straight away. He is going to leave it up though, because at some point the field will have the horses on it again and he's worried about rustlers.'

'I thought rustling was the sort of thing you see in those old cowboy films,' she said.

'It's alive and kicking in the UK,' Kit told her. 'Thousands of animals are stolen every year, apparently.'

'Oh, right.' She picked up her drink and took a sip. She wanted to say something witty or funny, but she felt a little tongue-tied.

'I was going to send you flowers as a thank you,' he continued, 'but I don't want it to become a habit.' He laughed, and Esther thought he sounded a little self-conscious.

'If you call sending me flowers once, a habit, then OK,' she teased, although she would secretly love to receive another bunch. There was something about getting flowers that made her feel incredibly special, even if they were just to say thanks and not "I love you".

'I've sent you flowers twice,' he said.

'I'm sorry? I thought you said, twice?'

'I did. The first time was to your flat after I returned your bag to you. Remember?'

Esther blinked in confusion. 'I don't follow...'

'You left your handbag in my car and I— oh Lord, please don't tell me I got the wrong address and left it outside someone else's door? I'm so sorry, but I watched you go into the building and when I brought your bag round the next day the lady in the downstairs flat said—'

'That was you?' Esther interrupted. No way. It couldn't be. She would have remembered. Wouldn't she? And what was he doing driving taxis? Did he need the extra income?

'So it *was* the right flat? Thank God for that!'

'*You* are the taxi driver?' She knew her voice had risen to a pitch only dogs could hear, but she was becoming slightly hysterical at the thought that she'd allowed Kit Reynolds to drive her home and then not recognised him. To be fair, she had drunk rather a lot, and she'd even managed to book a bloody holiday without realising it. But still…

'I thought you knew,' he said.

She buried her face in her hands and groaned. 'Sorry, I should have realised. I'd had a bit too much to drink,' she muttered, her voice muffled.

'Yeah, you had.'

She risked a peek through her fingers. He was laughing at her and she'd never felt so embarrassed in all her life. 'I honestly don't remember you. I hope I gave you a tip.'

He grinned. 'Nope, no tip.'

'Oh, I feel awful now. I'm generally a pretty good tipper, honest.' She took her hands away from her face. 'Next time I call a cab and it's you who's driving, I promise I won't be so mean.'

His mouth dropped open. 'Wait – you think I'm a taxi driver?'

'Aren't you?'

'No.' His eyes were crinkling in the corners and she had a horrible feeling there was more to this which she probably didn't want to hear.

'If you're not a taxi driver, why did you take me home? How did that happen?'

'You more or less jumped out in front of my car, leapt in the back and demanded I drive you home. You said there was a van after you.'

'Oh God.' She groaned again, wishing the ground would open up and swallow her. He must think she was a right looney. Or a complete idiot. Or both. 'I do remember booking a taxi,' she said slowly. 'No wait, come to think of it, maybe I booked the holiday instead.' That would explain why none of the taxi firms had had any record of her phone call, or her booking.

Kit barked out a laugh. 'You've got to explain.'

Yes, she supposed she better had, so haltingly and with lots of wincing and grimacing and feeling highly embarrassed, she told him the reason why she'd had too much to drink (Josh's fault) and why she'd thought that going on holiday to Malaga was a good idea (also Josh's fault). 'The page must have still been on my screen, and I saw the "pay now" button and thought I was booking a taxi. I'm so, so sorry.'

'Don't be. I think it's hilarious.'

'Thank you for returning my bag, and for the flowers.' She cringed. 'Both bouquets.'

'You're welcome. Now, shall we order?'

Esther's appetite had disappeared, along with her self-respect. How could she have made such a fool of herself?

She picked something light and hoped she could force it down. She wasn't in the habit of allowing her personal life and work to mix, but since Josh had absconded to Spain, she'd done nothing but blur the lines between the two. When he'd dumped her so thoughtlessly while she was in work, she hadn't been able to help her reaction, although she did feel guilty about all the times she'd disappeared off to the loo to check Flamingo Cam. But she honestly thought she'd moved past that since starting her job at LandScape.

Apparently not. she'd only gone and managed to mistake one of the company's owners for a taxi driver while drunk, had spent hours spying on him, and had sneaked into his garden and got caught. And now she was having lunch with him and she wasn't sure whether it constituted a date or not.

'You mentioned other webcams?' Kit said, and Esther mentally groaned again.

'Please can we change the subject?' she pleaded.

'Of course, but you've told me what happened and there was a perfectly logical explanation, so I don't see the problem. Or are there other ones out there that are similar?'

'No!' Crikey, she didn't want him to think she was some kind of voyeur (although that's exactly what she *was* doing, her conscience chirped up). She took a deep breath and said, 'It all started when my now ex boyfriend, Josh, called me from the airport to tell me he was moving to Spain and going to work in a bar called the Pink Flamingo.'

'You didn't know he was planning this?' Kit guessed, and she saw a flash of sympathy in his eyes.

She shook her head. 'Not an inkling. I was a bit upset.' That was the understatement of the year, she thought before carrying on. 'And I wanted to know more about where he was going and what he was doing, so I Googled it. The Pink Flamingo had a website…' She paused. 'They also had a camera pointing at the bar, and they're not the only ones. There are loads of places that have them, from small businesses to huge public places like Barcelona's main beach, and more obscure locations like a watering hole on the African plains.'

'You saw your ex on the webcam, didn't you?'

She looked away. 'Yes.'

'And you kept watching and torturing yourself,' he continued. The sympathy in his voice was back in spades.

She nodded. 'I don't look at it anymore,' she said. She didn't think it wise to confess that the reason she hadn't checked on Flamingo Cam for ages was because she'd been too busy watching him.

'That's good. It can't be healthy.'

Esther smiled at him, grateful that he understood. 'Exactly,' she said. 'I honestly don't care enough about Josh now to want to know what he gets up to.'

Kit's gaze was steady. 'You're over him, would you say?'

'Yes. Definitely.'

'Here's our food,' he said as one of the bar staff approached with a couple of plates, and to Esther's relief the conversation moved onto other things, and she found that Kit was good company, as he regaled her with stories of some of the clients he'd had and some of the gardens he'd transformed.

'She kept parading around in a bikini,' he was telling her, 'despite the fact it was February. She used to wear a robe over the top and let it fall open every time she saw me. I can't tell you how relieved I was to finish that particular job. For one, I don't date clients, and for another, she was about the same age as my mother.'

'Age shouldn't matter,' Esther retorted primly, just to wind him up.

'It doesn't, but she had a son older than me, and it simply didn't feel right. Besides, I didn't fancy her. She was too…' he hesitated, then finished with, 'high maintenance. Fake. Plastic almost.'

'False boobs?'

'Yep.'

'False nails?'

'Those, too.'

'How about a spray tan?'

'Right again. And she was constantly fiddling with her hair or checking herself out in the mirror.' Abruptly his face clouded over, and he speared a chip with more force than a fisherman wielding a harpoon.

What had brought that on, Esther wondered.

'Anyway, I won't bore you to death,' he said, after

he'd swallowed his mouthful of food. 'What about you? What made you decide to work at LandScape Ltd?'

'You sound like you're interviewing me,' she joked, thinking that she could listen to him talk for hours and never be bored.

'I might be.' His smile told her he was teasing. 'I didn't get a chance to do the real thing.'

'Oh, did you want to?' Esther was suddenly flustered. Should Dean have involved his brother in the interview process?

'No, although if I'd known it was you….' He left the rest of the sentence hanging and smirked at her.

'Stop it,' she groaned, putting her knife and fork down and pushing her plate away. 'Are we back to the taxi thing again, because if we are, I'm sure I've got something more important to do, like filing or shredding.'

'Actually, if we've both finished, I do have to pop into the office, so I'll walk you back.'

He insisted on paying the bill (which made the lunch feel even more like a date, in Esther's mind), and the pair of them slowly strolled out of the pub and onto the pavement. The green was bustling with children playing, their parents sitting on benches chatting, or supervising them on the swings, and older people were sitting around the pond enjoying the sunshine and feeding the ducks.

'I love this place,' Kit said.

'Actually, so do I,' Esther admitted. She didn't miss working in the city in the slightest. Her commute was shorter for a start – which was ironic considering Middlewick was a good few miles further away – and she loved the drive out to the village. She also looked forward to her lunchtime walk to the green, and being able to eat her sandwiches outside without the steady rumble of traffic or the smell of car fumes to keep her company. She much preferred the sound of squabbling ducks and the scent of freshly mown grass. Although whether she remained so enamoured of the place when the warm summer sun had given way to rain and icy wind, was a different matter. She was looking forward to autumn though, as she'd spotted a stile leading to a wooded area, and she couldn't wait to pop her boots on and kick through the fallen leaves.

She was coming to love this little village and the company she was working for.

She was also extremely attracted to the man at her side and could see herself falling for him if she wasn't careful which wouldn't be the sensible thing to do, considering the circumstances

It was with a mixture of dismay and relief that they parted company at Landscape's door – her to her desk and Kit to his office – but during the rest of the afternoon she was terribly conscious of his presence. It didn't help that he'd left his door open and she could see him pouring over some papers or working at his computer.

Annoyed with herself, Esther decided to do that shredding after all, as a form of punishment, but she couldn't help it if the shredder was only a few feet away from his office door, could she?

CHAPTER 38

'Oh, my, God!' Sinead nearly spat her drink out, laughing and coughing at the same time. 'I can't believe you showed him that!'

Esther had just finished telling her friends about how she'd managed to frighten Giles off by showing him Flamingo Cam.

'I think I'm going to wet myself.' Sinead leant into Ben, and Ben rolled his eyes.

'Please tell me you're joking?' he begged.

'Nope. I really did rabbit on and on about watching Josh live, then when I showed him some of the other sites, he went all weird on me and did a runner.'

'*He* went weird on *you*? Don't you think it's the other way around?' Sinead spluttered.

Esther giggled. 'I suppose so. What?' Charlie was giving her an odd look.

'I forgot to tell you. I showed Jay the photo you sent me of Giles, and he swore he knew the guy from the gym, so he did a little digging and found out some things about him. His real name isn't Giles, it's Clive, and he works for a firm of solicitors in Worcester. He's also married, and he's got three kids. Oh, and he doesn't live in Droitwich – he lives in Pershore.'

'Bloody hell!' Esther sat back in her seat in shock. 'No wonder he looked so worried when I told him about the webcams. He probably thought his wife might be spying on him, using the internet.'

'That's not all,' Charlie continued. 'Guess what he does for a living? Jay, tell her.' She nudged her boyfriend in the ribs.

'Huh?' Jay turned away from Steve who he'd been having a discussion with. 'What?'

'Tell Esther what that bloke she had a date with does for a living. You remember, the one who called himself Giles but whose real name is Clive.'

'Oh, him.' Jay chuckled. 'He's a lawyer, specialising in family law, mainly divorce.'

'Divorce! Hah!' Charlie echoed. 'And I bet you it's not the first time he's cheated on his wife, either. At the rate he's going he'll be representing himself soon enough.'

Esther was shaking her head. It was rather funny, after all. He hadn't been able to get away from her fast enough. Some good might come of it though, if it meant Giles/Clive stopped cheating on his wife. It wouldn't look very good to his clients would it, if the solicitor representing them was having to go to court himself.

'I've got more news,' she declared, joining in with the spirit of things. 'I've been on another date, this time with a guy called Robin. He works in insurance but apparently not in the boring car, house, pet sector. Oh no, he's some kind of specialist. Anyway, he was rather good looking and quite easy to talk to, so I wasn't going to hold that against him.' She paused for dramatic effect. 'What I did hold against him, was that he insisted on buying my drinks all night then expected me to go to bed with him.'

'What! That's disgusting!' Abbie looked appalled, and the others were in shock too.

'I hope you told him where to go,' Steve said. 'Let me have his number and I'll—'

'It's fine,' Esther interjected hastily. 'I'm a big girl and I can fight my own battles, and yes, I did tell him where to go.'

'Have you got any other dates lined up?' Charlie wanted to know after they'd all stopped spluttering with laughter. 'I hope so, because your love life is more entertaining than anything on TV.'

'Speaking of TVs, you'll never guess what else has

happened.' In for a penny in for a pound, she thought. At least her pathetic excuse for a love life was making her friends laugh. So she decided to tell them about Kit.

'Can you remember when I came to yours, had too much to drink, and booked a holiday by mistake?' she began, speaking to Charlie.

'You didn't!' Sinead exclaimed, looking from one to the other, her eyes wide.

'She did,' Charlie said. 'Jay and I went instead, because Esther couldn't go.'

'Now I get it. How was Malaga? Oh.' Sinead caught her lip between her teeth. 'Sorry,' she said to Esther.

'It's fine. I'm over Josh, although I still can't believe he knew I was watching him on the webcam. That's what I wanted to tell you. But I need to backtrack a bit. That night when I booked the holiday, I thought I was booking a taxi.'

'You weren't?' Abbie was trying not to laugh.

'No. But I thought I was, and when this car slowed down, I assumed it was my taxi, so I got in it and insisted that the man drove me home. Thankfully he did, but I left my bag on the backseat. He returned it to me the next day, and then a few days later he sent me flowers with a note asking if I wanted to go out for a drink.'

'And did you?'

'No, because I couldn't remember what he looked like.' She didn't tell her friends that she had phoned him since; they didn't need to know how desperate she'd been or how lonely. 'There's more. You know I was a bit obsessed with looking at the Pink Flamingo?'

'A bit? Don't you mean, a lot?' Charlie rolled her eyes.

Esther ignored her. 'One day, another webcam popped up on my screen, but this one didn't show a bar, or a beach, or a famous square – it showed the back of someone's house.'

'No! Do you know whose it was?'

'Not then, but I do now. It belongs to Dean's brother.'

'Kit Reynolds?' Steve asked, and Esther recalled that the reason she'd met Dean in the first place was because Steve and Abbie had thought it a good idea to invite him along as a blind date for her.

'The very same.' She grimaced. 'I only found out because I spotted a photo of Kit in work and thought that the man on the screen looked like him. I knew where he lived, so the other evening I sneaked into his garden to check.'

'And?' That was from Jay, but all her friends were also hanging on her next word.

'He caught me,' she said.

'Oh, my God! What did he do?' Sinead leant forward in her seat. 'Did he have you arrested.'

'No! He was quite nice about it, once I'd explained. But the awful thing is, he's actually my boss. Dean hired me, but they run the company equally. And that's not all.' She began to laugh so hard she could hardly get the words out. 'He was the guy who gave me a lift home because I dived into his car thinking it was a taxi!'

'Flipping heck! You couldn't make this stuff up. Talk about a coincidence.' That was from Ben, who up to now hadn't said a great deal. He'd just sat there, shaking his head in disbelief. 'Fate seems to be throwing the two of you together.'

Esther was pleased she'd made her friends laugh, but when she thought about Giles/Clive and Robin, she felt quite despondent. Were there any men out there who weren't complete gits? Present company excepted, of course. She couldn't imagine any of her friends behaving so badly. At least Josh hadn't cheated on her, but he had lied though in a way, making her believe they were happy together when he so clearly hadn't been. But before him, she'd gone out with a guy called Liam and he'd turned out to be untrustworthy because he'd also cheated on her with a girl who worked in the hairdressers on Stratford

Road.

An awful thought occurred to her; maybe it wasn't them, but her. She understood that the men were to blame for being unfaithful (she couldn't carry the can for their lack of morals) but the fact that she seemed to attract that sort of fella must surely be a reflection on her. Maybe she was giving out the wrong sort of vibes?

Was there anyone out there who wasn't already taken and was a nice guy?

She bloody well hoped so otherwise she might as well give up on love now and buy herself a dozen cats.

But one thought continued to haunt her for the rest of the evening – Kit was a nice guy, wasn't he?

CHAPTER 39

'She can ask, but that doesn't necessarily mean she'll get it,' Nash explained after Kit told him about Nancy's latest demand. 'The law *can* order someone to financially maintain their former spouse even after divorce or dissolution. In short, there is a common law duty imposed upon spouses to support each other whilst the marriage or civil partnership exists but what many people aren't aware of is, that the duty may continue after the marriage is dissolved. The entitlement isn't automatic, but the court must consider whether the one spouse needs a regular income from the other in addition to the division of assets.'

'But she didn't contribute anything to the house, and certainly not to the business,' Kit objected. 'I'm not being mean and I don't want to see her homeless, but honestly…'

'OK, the principle behind spousal maintenance is to meet the ongoing reasonable financial needs of the financially weaker party, such as a wife giving up work to look after their children. There are plenty of examples, I've just picked one at random, and I know this particular circumstance doesn't apply to your situation, but Nancy did give up work.'

'Because she *wanted* to, not because she *had* to. She said she wanted to take some time to decide what she wanted to do with her life. The "some time" turned into "a lot of time". I don't believe she had any intention of working ever again, not when I was earning enough to support both of us. Don't get me wrong,' Kit added hastily, 'I was more than happy for her to not work. As long as she was happy, that was all that mattered to me. But she can hardly claim that she can't find a job now, can she?'

'That's for the court to decide and although I agree with you, we'll just have to wait and see.'

Kit sighed heavily. He wasn't a particularly impatient man, but this was dragging on and on. And the not-knowing was slowly destroying him. Which was why he kept asking Dean to sort out a package, in case things didn't go the way Kit hoped. The worst-case scenario was that he'd have to sell his home and lose his share of the business. The best case was that he'd get to keep both. He was realistic enough to know that the outcome would be somewhere in the middle, but if it came to a choice between his beloved cottage and the company which he'd helped create from nothing, then he wasn't sure which way the dice would fall.

It was only after he'd said his goodbyes to Nash Layton and was heading out to an architectural salvage yard to look for something old and unusual for a client in Upton Snodsbury, that he realised he did, in fact know, which choice he'd make.

'Sorry, Dean…' he muttered.

CHAPTER 40

Esther looked up from her computer as the door opened and she saw Kit coming through it, a smile on his face. Her heart did a little jump at the sight of him. It had been doing that a lot lately. Just thinking about him was enough to make it skip a beat.

She must stop this. Having the hots for your boss wasn't to be recommended even if he was gorgeous and funny, and nice and charming, and an all-round decent guy. Dating anyone you worked with was never a good idea – if things didn't work out, what happened then?

At best there would probably be an awkward atmosphere.

At worst, she might be forced to look for another job if this one became untenable, and she certainly didn't want to do that. She loved working at LandScape Ltd; she'd settled in and had got to grips with the admin and was starting to make a difference in terms of how the place ran. Everything was better organised and more streamlined, and as she gained an increased understanding, she was able to take on greater responsibility therefore freeing Dean up to do more important things, like finding more clients.

'Good afternoon, Friday,' Kit said, nodding a greeting.

'Good afternoon, Mr Reynolds.'

Kit's grin widened. 'You can call me Kit, you know. We don't stand on ceremony here.'

Her reaction to his greeting had been an instinctive one to try to distance herself from him emotionally. If she thought of him as Mr Reynolds, then she wouldn't be thinking of him as the Kit whose garden she'd been caught in, or the Kit who'd bought her lunch.

She'd also not be thinking of him as the man who she'd watched taking his T-shirt off, or cooking, or the man who she'd witnessed banging his hand against his door and looking so sad and angry that her heart had gone out to him.

So, it would have to be Mr Reynolds from now on.

It was a shame that the only nice bloke she'd met in… well… forever, was the very one who was off-limits.

'I think I'll stick with Mr Reynolds,' she told him.

'Even if I call you Esther and not Friday?'

'You can call me whatever you like,' she said. 'Within reason.'

He tilted his head to the side and studied her. Esther returned to her screen and tried to pretend he wasn't there, which was rather difficult since she could smell his fresh citrussy aftershave, and his gaze felt as solid as a finger caressing her cheek. Her face grew hot and she knew she was blushing. She was so skin-tinglingly aware of him that her stomach was doing somersaults and she kept hitting the wrong keys, having to press delete so often that she was sure he knew she was making a pig's ear of the report she was trying to prepare for Dean.

Dean! Ah! That was her chance of getting him to leave her alone. 'Er, Dean's in his office, if you'd like to go through.'

'I'd prefer to stay here.'

What was she supposed to say to that? Was he flirting with her? Or did he mean that he didn't want to speak to Dean. She knew they were having a few differences of opinion, although she didn't know what it was about.

She risked a swift look. He was still smiling at her. It wasn't the teasing grin of a few minutes ago though. It was an altogether much softer expression. Hurriedly, she returned to her computer and the stupid keys which seemed to be jumping around and refusing to stay still.

That was another thing. Should she tell Dean about the webcam and how Kit – Mr Reynolds, she amended quickly – had found her prowling about in his garden?

He should be told. She didn't want to keep that kind of thing from him because if he found out he'd wonder why she hadn't mentioned it and that could lead to all sorts of things, and maybe he'd even begin to question her integrity and honesty.

'Will you please go away,' she said eventually, his nearness rattling her. 'I can't work with you staring at me. What do you want, anyway?'

'For you to go out to dinner with me.' He stopped and blinked, and Esther had the feeling that he hadn't meant to say what he'd just said.

She inhaled sharply, then let it out in a long sigh. 'Do you honestly think that's a good idea?' She needed to take the bull by the horns here, and spell it out to him.

'Probably not.'

It was Esther's turn to be surprised. 'Then why ask me?'

'I don't know.'

'That's not very flattering – *you don't know*.'

'I mean, I do know – because you're funny, and

pretty, and I like talking to you. But…'

'Exactly!'

'You don't know what I was going to say.'

'I do. You were going to say that as my employer, you shouldn't be asking me out.'

'I shouldn't?'

'No. It's not right. It could be construed as sexual harassment.'

Kitt took a step back. 'My apologies,' he said after a pause. 'My intention wasn't to make you feel uncomfortable.' He began to walk toward the exit, his car keys in his hand.

'You don't,' she called after him. The last thing she wanted was for him to think she was accusing him of something so awful. She wasn't. She was just trying to…? Actually, she wasn't entirely sure what she was trying to do, apart from ensuring she didn't make an idiot of herself by dating the boss when it would undoubtedly end in tears. Hers.

He halted and slowly turned to face her. 'I don't?'

'No.'

It was his turn to ask, 'Then why…?'

'Because you can't go around chatting up the hired help,' she explained. 'Some women might take it the wrong way.'

He stiffened again and drew himself up. He *was* quite tall, she thought absently, recalling her previous impression of him as being at least six foot. Her guess had been correct.

'Do you seriously think I make a habit of asking my staff out?' he demanded. 'Because I don't.'

'I never said you did.'

'You implied it. I'll have you know that you're the first woman I've asked out to dinner since—' He stopped abruptly, and Esther wondered what he'd been about to say. 'Never mind.' He marched toward the door, his back rigid. Gone was the easy confidence that he'd exuded a few minutes ago and she knew she'd offended him.

Oh God, now she felt awful. 'OK, yes,' she called as he yanked the door open with enough force to nearly jerk it off its hinges. He must have done the exact same thing when she ended up in the planter, she realised, wondering if he made a habit of storming out of LandScape's offices.

He halted. 'Yes what?' he asked over his shoulder, without turning around to look at her.

'Yes, please?' The words were out of her mouth before she had a chance to think about them. She felt like a five-year-old being chastised for bad manners and she instantly wished she could take them back. Was she supposed to feel grateful that he'd asked her out to dinner?

He turned to face her, and she saw a small smile

playing about his lips. 'I meant, what are you saying yes to?'

Ah. 'Dinner.'

'Good. If you're sure?'

She wasn't. 'I am.'

'Tonight?'

'Erm…?' Crikey, that was quick – she felt she needed time to process things.

'Another night, then?'

'Tonight is fine.' How much time did she need? If she was going to do this, and she clearly was, then tonight was as good a night as any to go against her principles and her common sense. What was the point of delaying it?

'I hope you don't think I'm taking advantage of you?' He looked nervous and slightly worried.

'I don't.' She was telling the truth. She didn't think he was the type to use his position to get her to go out with him. Now Robin, on the other hand, would probably do exactly that!

'Because if you do—?' he continued hesitantly.

'I don't,' she repeated.

'I know a nice place near Abberton. Shall I meet you there, or would you like me to pick you up?'

'I'll meet you there.' After her last couple of disastrous dates, she wanted to be able to do a runner if necessary. Although this situation was a trifle different in that she knew she'd have to see him again, no matter how well or how badly the evening went.

Oh, dear – what was she letting herself in for?

***

Oh dear, what had he let himself in for? And, to make matters worse, until he'd driven off Kit had forgotten what he'd come into the office for. It certainly hadn't been to ask Esther out. He had wanted to speak to Dean about a proposal which might solve his immediate problems, but in hindsight maybe he'd leave it for a few days. There was nothing definite yet, so until he had something concrete to report there wasn't any point in worrying his brother unduly. Besides, Kit needed to talk to some people first, and then he'd have to go through the interview process, and being invited to an interview didn't necessarily mean he'd get the job.

Actually, thinking about it, asking Esther out (where those words had come from, he had no idea) had saved Dean a lot of worry. Because Dean undoubtedly *would* worry, Kit knew. He'd also try to talk him out of it, so maybe Kit asking Esther to dinner was his way of subconsciously avoiding a confrontation with Dean.

He couldn't believe she'd thought he made a habit

of asking his employees out, but he could see why she might think that way. You had to be so careful, and quite rightly too. He didn't want her to think he was taking advantage of her and that she didn't have any choice in the matter if she wanted to keep her job. And he might have retracted the offer in the light of what she'd said if it wasn't for the fact that his plans might come to fruition, and would solve the problem not only of Nancy but also of his being Esther's boss. Even if this opportunity didn't work out, there'd be others.

And with that, Kit found he was looking forward to his date with Esther, because that's what it was – a date. It wasn't two colleagues meeting over a meal. It wasn't two friends on an evening out together. This was a proper date, and for the first time in months he felt that his life was looking up.

CHAPTER 41

What should she wear? Nothing too officey that's for sure, although if she did it might reinforce the message that dating the hired help wasn't a good idea. Although, she reasoned, it was probably too late to back-track now. Esther knew what she had been agreeing to when she said yes to dinner, and she wasn't under any illusion that this was a business meeting or that he'd asked her because he wanted to become her new BFF. This was a date. And her heart was in her mouth and her stomach was doing somersaults at the thought of it. Crikey, she was a mess!

And she still didn't know what she was going to wear. She shouldn't have agreed to see him tonight, it was too soon. She needed time to pop out and buy something. She needed time to shave her legs and armpits, paint her toenails, and put a facemask on. As it was, all she had time for was a shower, renew her make-up (not that she ever wore much) and desperately root around in her wardrobe for something that wasn't too smart, yet wasn't too far into the baggy T-shirt and leggings league.

After much debating and having tried on everything she owned at least twice (including the dress she only ever wore with thick black tights and winter boots) she settled on a pretty summer dress in burnt orange, her leather jacket (in case the temperature dropped a little later on) and a pair of gladiator sandals. As she was putting them on, she ran a hand up her shin and was relieved to discover there were no yeti hairs sprouting out of her legs.

Then she gave herself a stern talking to – no matter how attracted she was to Kit, he wasn't going to get close enough to even *see* any hair on her legs, let alone feel it, so it didn't matter whether she'd shaved them or not. And rather than taking off the old nail varnish on her toes, she swiped a fresh coat over the top and told herself it would have to do. He'd have to take her or leave her. She wished she could be like Clara, the sleek, polished girl whom she'd briefly worked with in the bank, but no matter how much she tried, Esther couldn't seem to manage to achieve the same degree of sophistication.

Grabbing her bag and her keys, she dashed out of

the door with half an hour to spare. It should be plenty of time to drive to the pub, but she hated being late even if it was supposed to be fashionable and the done thing.

Kit was already there, she saw, as she drove into the carpark and spotted his 4x4. It was another tick in the box of the things she liked about him. He was on time. He'd also ordered a drink for her, she discovered when she joined him at the table; sparkling water, the same drink she'd chosen when they'd had lunch, although he did offer to fetch her something else from the bar if she wanted. It was nice that he'd remembered. It was also nice that he hadn't bought her an alcoholic drink in order to have an excuse to drive her home, which was what another man (she inserted the name Robin, here) might have done.

'Have you always lived in Worcester?' Kit asked once they'd settled down.

'Yes, born and bred there. How about you?' She already knew that his and Dean's parents owned a farm and that the LandScape offices once used to be a selection of barns, but she wondered if he'd lived anywhere else in between.

'I've always lived in Middlewick,' he said, leaning back in his seat and crossing his legs at the ankles. He looked relaxed and confident. He also hadn't taken his eyes off her, and his attention was giving her a warm, tingly feeling. 'I can't imagine living anywhere else.' A shadow flitted across his face but was gone so quickly she wasn't sure it had actually been there.

'It is lovely,' she agreed. 'So peaceful. It's only a few miles from the city centre yet it could be a hundred. I envy you.'

'You do? Wouldn't you miss the bright lights and the buzz?'

Esther laughed. 'This is Worcester we're talking about,' she giggled, 'not London. There *are* no bright lights. As far as cities go, it's rather old-fashioned and genteel.'

'True, but it does have some nightlife, and then there's the café culture and the shopping…?'

'I actually like not working in the city,' she admitted. 'I prefer Middlewick.'

'It's not all summer breezes and picnics on the green,' he pointed out. 'You wait until the snow is down and your car gets stuck in a drift.'

'You'll just have to tow me out, won't you?' she teased.

'I'm serious,' he said. 'If you think you're not going to make it into work, give me a shout and I'll come and fetch you. We rarely have really bad weather, so my car should be able to handle it.'

At least he assumed that she'd still be working for LandScape Ltd come the winter, she mused. Maybe the notion that relationships in the workplace were a bad idea, hadn't occurred to him. Although, there were husband and wife teams who worked well together – take Drew Pritchard and his wife Rebecca from that TV programme Salvage Hunters, for instance. But then, there was the question of whether they'd formed the business together, or whether it had been his and she'd simply slotted into it. There was quite a bit of difference between the two and—

Slow down and back up a little, she told herself. This was just a date. It wasn't as though he'd asked her to marry him and join him in running the business. She was letting her imagination run away with her. She might be more than ready to find love again now that Josh was out of her heart and her mind, but there were many steps between dating and falling in love, and between falling in love and getting married. She and Kit had taken a baby step, and right now she wasn't sure there was going to be another one.

They spent the rest of the evening chatting easily. She felt comfortable in his company and she thought he might feel the same about being with her, especially since they kept catching each other's eye and smiling. Once, while they were waiting for their dessert, she and Kit had shared a long, lingering look and her tummy had tingled with excitement. Until the waitress had appeared and the mood was broken, that is.

Esther hadn't known whether to be relieved or disappointed. The more time she spent in Kit's company, the more she was growing to like him. She already fancied him rotten (she had done so since the moment he'd taken his T-shirt off – perhaps even before then), but now that she was getting to know him as a person, she found she more than liked him. He was fun to be with and easy to talk to, but he had a serious side to him too, she discovered when he talked passionately about what gardens and gardening meant to him. She only wished she felt as deeply about something, and she found she was rather envious.

But the tipping point came when it was time to get into their respective cars.

'I enjoyed this evening,' Kit said as they strolled slowly across the car park.

Esther didn't want the evening to end – she'd had such a nice time – but now that they were about to say goodnight, she was suddenly all-aflutter. Would he kiss her? Would he get in his car and drive off? Or would he shake her hand?

Their cars were parked side-by-side and he walked her around to her driver side and waited while she aimed the key fob at it. The car chirped into life.

'Right, then,' she said awkwardly. 'I'll... um... see you soon.'

'You most certainly will,' he agreed, making no move to unlock his own car. She was acutely aware of how close he was. There was barely a couple of feet between them, and his nearness was doing funny things to her heart rate.

Slowly, so very slowly, he closed the small gap between them, then he leant forward, bent his head, and she simply knew he was going to kiss her and—

Oh....

His lips were warm and soft as they grazed her own, and her eyelids fluttered closed as she gave herself to the wonderful sensations coursing through her.

Without her even realising, he'd wrapped his arms around her and drew her to him, until she was melting into his embrace.

'Wow,' he said softly, when they finally parted.

Esther wasn't sure she could take any more, but neither was she sure she wanted the kiss to end. Her heart was pounding and her knees were shaking, and she wasn't entirely certain that her legs could hold her upright for much longer. It was lucky his arms were still around her, otherwise she might fall over.

'Yeah, wow,' she breathed, then tilted her chin for him to kiss her again.

This time they were lost to the world for several wonderful, delicious minutes. He tasted divine, and the way he nibbled her lips was intoxicating. She felt as though she'd drunk some magic potion which filled her to the brim with the taste, the feel, and the scent of him. She could have stayed in his arms forever if it hadn't been for the floodlights in the pub's car park coming on and illuminating them in sharp relief.

They pulled apart quickly, almost guiltily, and Esther gave a small self-conscious giggle.

'Look at us,' he said, 'behaving like a couple of teenagers.' His voice was gruff, sending shivers down her spine to add to all the other sensations washing through her.

She was a mess, and she'd loved every second of it.

'I'd like to see you again. May I?' Kit lifted his hand and stroked her cheek with his finger, sending a delicious shiver down her back.

Not trusting herself to speak, she nodded.

'Good.' His head dipped once more and she thought he was going to kiss her again and her lips parted in anticipation, but all he did was plant a chaste peck on her forehead.

Darn it!

'There's um…. something…' he began, then hesitated.

'What?'

He smiled down at her. 'It doesn't matter. What are you doing on Saturday?'

'Nothing.' She decided to be honest. What was the point in pretending she was busy?

'Would you like to spend the night with me?'

'*Excuse me?*'

He threw his head back and laughed. 'That came out wrong, although…? Sorry, what I meant to say was, would you like to spend the night star gazing? If you fancy a bit of a hike, we can visit the Malvern Hills. It's the best place around here for seeing stars.'

Oh, I don't know, Esther thought to herself. *I think I might have seen some when you kissed me.* 'That sounds wonderful.'

'We can take a picnic and eat it on the top. It will mean quite a late night though, because it doesn't get properly dark until ten o'clock, or even later. We could get there early enough to watch the sunset. What do you think?'

Esther thought it sounded simply wonderful.

CHAPTER 42

Kit packed his rucksack with care. There was a little delicatessen in the village which also doubled as a bakers, and he made a point of visiting it early that morning before all the good stuff had gone, and he was pleased with the selection of food that he was now placing delicately into his bag. He'd take a blanket to sit on and another to wrap Esther up in if she got cold. It might be the middle of summer but lying on your back on the top of the Malvern Hills at night probably wouldn't be the warmest place he could take her on a date.

It was the most romantic place he could think of though, and the thought of being alone with her for a few hours made his heart sing. He hadn't been able to get their kiss out of his head. Not that he wanted to. He'd thoroughly enjoyed every second of it and couldn't wait to do it again. She'd felt so right in his arms, as though she'd been made to be there.

He adored everything about her – the way she looked (gorgeous and cute and sexy all at the same time), the way she smelled (of flowers and vanilla), the way she felt (small and delicate as she let herself be held by him). There wasn't a thing he didn't like, and he found it difficult to believe that she'd burrowed her way under his skin so quickly. Not too long ago he'd been telling himself that he couldn't face another relationship so soon after Nancy, yet here he was happily preparing to take another woman on a romantic night out. Or what he hoped would be a romantic night – she might hate having to trek up a fairly big hill, eat with her fingers, with only the stars and his scintillating company for entertainment.

Nancy would have loathed it.

Speaking of Nancy, he'd almost confessed to Esther that he was still married, but something had held him back. He wasn't sure how she'd react, and they'd been having such a lovely time (ooh, those kisses) that he hadn't wanted to spoil things. He'd tell her later, he vowed; not later tonight, but further into their relationship. If it petered out between them, then it didn't matter whether he'd told her or not. But if things progressed the way he hoped they would, he wanted to make sure there was more of a commitment between them before he told her about the existence of a soon-to-be ex-wife. He didn't want to frighten her off at this early stage, not when they were just getting to know each other. Besides, by leaving it a few weeks, he might have a better idea of how much longer it would be before the divorce was finalised, what his financial situation might be, and whether he was going to be made homeless or jobless. Actually, the job thing might not be so much of an issue—

Damn it! Look at the time. He needed to shift his backside if they were to reach the top of the Worcestershire Beacon in time to watch the sun sink behind the distant Welsh hills. He'd checked the forecast (several times and somewhat obsessively) and he was pleased to see the weather report was for clear skies this evening. Perfect!

He pressed the buzzer for the top flat and heard Esther come racing down the stairs, and when she opened the door he was relieved to see she was dressed sensibly in sturdy trainers, jeans, and a puffer jacket.

'You told me to dress warmly,' she said. 'But can I take my jacket off while we're in the car – I'm sweltering.'

'You might not need it at all,' he advised, his pulse gearing up a notch as she wriggled out of the jacket and popped it on the back seat. She was wearing a fleece, and decided to take that off too, and he had to look away as she dragged it over her head, her T-shirt riding up to reveal an expanse of flat tummy.

'That's better,' she said, strapping herself in and settling back in her seat. 'How long do you think it'll take to reach the top of the Beacon? I haven't been up there since I was a kid.'

'About two hours.'

'All uphill?'

He caught her biting her lip. 'It's a steady incline, rather than a steep climb,' he told her. 'You'll be fine, and you've got a picnic to look forward to at the end of it.'

'I hope you've brought loads, because I'm going to be seriously hungry.'

He laughed. 'I have, I promise, and if you're still hungry by the time we get back to the car later, I'll buy you fish and chips.'

'You know how to treat a girl,' she said, and her eyes were full of laughter so he knew she was teasing. If Nancy had made a comment like that, it would have been dripping with sarcasm. Nancy didn't care much for the outdoors, and the idea of eating fish and chips while sitting in the car would have sent her into hysterics.

Stop it, he admonished silently – he really must stop comparing Esther to Nancy, even if Nancy did come off worse every single time. He must stop thinking about Nancy altogether, but Esther was such a refreshing change that he couldn't help it. He was surprised though, to realise that his thoughts of Nancy weren't tinged with the usual despair and sadness. He was finally able to think about her quite rationally and dispassionately, and he knew he was finally over her. As soon as the divorce came through he could carry on with the rest of his life.

There was one thing he knew, though – he thought he might like Esther to be in it with him and he smiled.

'What are you smiling about?' she asked, breaking into his reverie.

'Nothing, I'm just happy.'

She turned her head to look at him and he shot her a quick glance, hoping he wasn't coming on too strong. 'Me, too,' she said, and his heart did a kind of flip-flop.

God, he wanted to pull over right now and kiss her again.

Instead, he concentrated on the road, and tried to bring his racing pulse down to a level where he didn't think he was about to have a heart attack.

They travelled in companionable silence for a while, until Kit pulled into the car park. Esther got out and reached for her fleece and her jacket. He had to force himself to look away when she put the fleece back on, and he pretended to adjust the straps on the rucksack so she didn't see him staring at her. He only stopped messing with his rucksack when he saw her tying her jacket around her waist.

'Ready?' he asked.

She nodded and took a deep breath of clean air. 'It's still so warm,' she observed.

'You'll get warmer as we begin to climb,' he warned, 'but when we get to the top and sit still for a while, it might get quite chilly.'

'Do you do this often?'

'Take women on gruelling hikes up mountains and force them to star-gaze with me? No, you're the first.'

'Didn't any of your other girlfriends fancy it?'

'I've never asked anyone else to come with me, and no, I don't come up here often. It's beautiful and humbling, but it can also be quite lonely without someone to share the experience with.'

He felt a light touch on his arm. Esther's face was full of empathy.

'I know what that's like,' she said. 'I also know that if you're sharing it with the wrong person, that can be lonely too.'

Kit's breath caught in his throat. Should he tell her about Nancy now? This was the perfect opportunity. He was sure she'd understand.

Or maybe not. Why risk spoiling what could be a wonderful evening?

They fell in side by side and began walking, chatting about nothing in particular at first, but when the track steepened Esther wasn't quite so talkative. Neither, for that matter, was Kit. He might have a relatively active job, but gardening wasn't in the same league as hiking up a rather large hill. But he knew the views from the top were worth it, so he kept going even though he would have preferred to lay the blanket down on the next flattish spot they came to. He'd promised her a sunset and stars, and by gosh, that's what he'd give her.

Finally, after several halts to catch their breath and much puffing and panting, they reached the top.

'Four hundred and twenty-five metres,' Kit announced, a little breathlessly as they reached the stone toposcope at the summit of the Beacon which showed all the notable landmarks that could be seen from that point.

Esther turned in a slow circle. 'There's Worcester Cathedral,' she said, pointing. 'And that must be Hereford.'

Kit pointed to another distant tower. 'I think that one is Gloucester Cathedral and look, you can see the Bristol Channel! We're lucky it's so clear this evening.'

Kit led her a short distance away from the summit

proper and they found a nice spot facing west and the rapidly setting sun, in which to spread the blanket out. While he unpacked his rucksack and the goodies it contained, Esther sat with her knees drawn up to her chest, her arms wrapped around them, and gazed at the spectacular view. Kit joined her on the blanket and they spent the next twenty minutes watching the sun going down, shoulders touching, watching one of nature's finest displays in awed silence.

'It's beautiful,' she whispered once, staring out at the almost black mountains in the distance with the sun blazing a deep orange behind them. Above them, the sky was the most magnificent shade of turquoise, gradually darkening to deep blue then navy in the east as the sun slipped below the horizon.

Before the light totally fled from the sky and once the magnificent colours of the sunset had faded, Kit suggested they eat while they were still able to see what they were eating.

'Good idea, I'm starving,' Esther said, studying the packets spread out on the blanket. 'What have we got?'

'Breadsticks, cheese, melon and strawberry skewers, chicken wraps, those things there are slices of mushroom strudel, that's asparagus and ricotta tart, and those are gorgonzola, pear and walnut pies. And I've brought some sparkling apple juice, oh, and a punnet of cherries.'

'My, that looks and sounds wonderful,' she said, as he handed her a paper plate and a napkin.

'Tuck in and, as I said, if you're still hungry afterwards…'

'I'm sure I won't be,' she said, helping herself to a slice of the mushroom strudel and one of the pies and diving in with enthusiasm.

That was another thing he liked about her – she wasn't scared of food. She had a healthy appetite and didn't pick and prod at what was on her plate. Unlike some people he didn't want to mention.

By the time it was fully dark and the first stars were becoming visible (although Jupiter – or was it Mars? – had been twinkling away in the east for a while now), they'd polished off most of the food Kit had brought with him.

He was lying out on the blanket, propped up on his elbows, and Esther was doing the same, neither of them saying much, simply enjoying the magic of the evening. He didn't feel the need to fill every quiet moment with chatter. Having her beside him was enough, and he realised he enjoyed her silence as much as he enjoyed it when they talked.

One by one, little pinpricks of light filled the sky until there were thousands of them, sparkling like jewels in the void above.

Esther scooted down until she was lying totally flat, her eyes wide and filled with wonder, and Kit found himself watching her instead of looking up. He thought she was more beautiful than the night, her features softer than the velvety darkness, and he wondered where such romantic sentiments were coming from.

'Fancy a cherry?' he asked, trying to distance himself from his unsettling thoughts and bring himself back down to earth.

'Hmm,' she murmured. 'I would, but I can't be bothered to move.'

Kit reached for one of the glossy red orbs and leant towards her. When Esther closed her eyes and opened her lips, he thought he'd never seen anything so desirable in his life.

He slipped the cherry into her mouth and watched as she slowly chewed.

She opened her lips for another, and this time, as he was about to pop it into her mouth, he noticed that her eyes were open and she was staring at him with an inscrutable expression.

He leant closer and closer, falling in the depths of her, until his lips met hers with the softest of touches.

Tentatively at first, but with growing intensity, they kissed until they were both breathless, their arms and legs entwined, their bodies pressed close together. Kit wanted to stay like this forever, holding her in his arms, kissing her sweet lips, feeling her gentle breath on his cheek and her soft curves against him. But eventually they drew apart and he cradled her head on his shoulder, drew the spare blanket around their shoulders, and lay back to watch the stars, letting the enchantment of the night flow over them.

CHAPTER 43

Esther's lids fluttered open and she lay there for a moment trying to get her bearings. Kit, stars, mountain tops… Last night flooded back to her and she realised that they were still on the hill, wrapped like a burrito in the blanket, snuggled together for warmth, and Kit was still fast asleep.

She took a minute to study him, the firm line of his jaw, his absurdly long lashes (far too long for a man – it wasn't fair, and why hadn't she noticed them before now), his aquiline nose, the way strands of his hair flopped over his forehead, the beginning of stubble on his chin.

Lying there, his arms firmly around her, she couldn't believe she'd spent the night with him. Not in the usual sense, but in the falling asleep sense. They'd kissed a lot, they'd watched the almost imperceptible wheel of the stars above them, they'd kissed some more, then they must have fallen asleep.

What a wonderful night she thought, feeling relaxed and absurdly happy. She also felt closer to him than she'd ever felt to anyone before, including Josh. Just the thought of Kit sent shivers of delight coursing through her.

She wanted to stay there forever on the mountain top, to hold him for the rest of their lives and never let him go. But dawn had broken, the sun was rising and soon their little piece of paradise would be awash with hikers.

Marvelling that she'd spent her first ever night outdoors and hadn't been cold once, she felt the early sun's warm rays on her face and stretched languidly. She didn't want to move and she certainly didn't want to break the spell, but she was stiff and she'd lost the circulation in one arm.

Kit stirred, and she gazed at him with an equal mixture of fascination and dread as he opened his eyes. Would his first reaction when he realised that they'd spent the night together be one of dismay?

With trepidation she watched as his gaze focused on her and the relief when a huge smile spread across his face almost took her breath away. He didn't regret it, and she was so happy she could cry.

'Are you OK?' he asked, worry creeping into his eyes.

'I'm fine,' she said, smiling at him. 'More than fine, actually. Last night was amazing.'

'It was, wasn't it? I told you this was one of the best places around here for star-gazing.'

She paused, sobering. 'I wasn't talking about the stars,' she said hesitantly.

'Weren't you?'

'No.'

'Good. I thought it was wonderful too. *You're* wonderful.'

Warmth that had nothing to do with the sun, surged through her and she knew she was blushing furiously. 'So are you,' she murmured.

Crikey, what had happened to them last night? Anyone would think they'd had a night of passion, when all they'd done was to kiss a bit (a lot, actually) and had then fallen asleep. They were behaving as though something much more profound had taken place.

Then again, maybe it had…

'Come on,' he said, scrambling to his feet and holding his hand out to haul her up. 'We need some breakfast.'

'Is that all you think about? Food?'

He gathered her to him and stared down at her. 'Not all, no. Not since I met you.' He kissed her on the nose. 'To be fair, I did think about other things too.' His lips parted and she couldn't take her eyes off them. 'But I can't for the life of me remember what they were,' he added. 'What have you done to me, Friday?'

Oh, God, she thought she might be about to explode from happiness. It wasn't quite a declaration of undying love, but he obviously had some feelings for her.

She had some feelings for him too. More than some. And she couldn't believe that she'd fallen so heavily for him in such a short space of time. She hardly knew him, but she felt a connection to him that went deeper than anything she'd experienced before.

A niggle of worry about what they were doing (he was still her boss) and how fast things were happening crossed her mind, but she pushed it away firmly. What will be, will be, she told herself philosophically. If this was meant to happen, then it will. If things fell apart then at least she'd given this wonderful burgeoning relationship a chance. The last thing she wanted to do now, after last night, was to have any regrets. And she had to ask herself what she would regret the most, walking away before anything more serious happened between them such as getting her heart broken or losing her job? Or giving love a chance and discovering that he might be her soul mate, and even if he wasn't and their relationship went nowhere, it didn't mean she'd have to give up her job, or if she did she could always find another.

'What are you thinking?' he asked, concern written all over his face.

'Let me cook you dinner tonight,' she blurted. It wouldn't be as delicious as the picnic, and the location wouldn't be as spectacular, but they were certain of being alone together. Should anything happen. Which it might. Or might not. She hadn't decided. Would it be too soon? Would he even want to? Maybe they needed more time to get to know each other first?

He hesitated, and she wondered if he knew what she was tentatively offering (she still wasn't sure) and he didn't approve. Was she coming on too strong? Too needy?

'I'd love to,' he said. 'But first, breakfast.'

'No, first this,' and she reached up to kiss him, and kept kissing him until she saw stars for the second time.

CHAPTER 44

Esther still wasn't decided. She'd been in a quandary for the whole day, trying to decide. The fact that she felt she had to make a decision wasn't helping her to make that decision. Should she ask him to stay the night? Could she? Was it too soon? Would he still feel the same way about her tomorrow if he did spend the night with her? How did he feel about her anyway?

She couldn't tell. She thought he really liked her, but it might be wishful thinking on her part, and maybe she was projecting her own growing feelings onto him. To Kit, she might simply be a casual fling for all she knew. She didn't think so, but…

'Give it a rest,' she muttered aloud, becoming heartily sick of trying to second guess herself. What had happened to that que será, será attitude of this morning?

Ah, *this morning*… waking up next to Kit had been

the best thing that had happened to her in ages. Then there were all those wonderful kisses, both last night and earlier today. And they'd had breakfast together in a little café in Malvern, giggling like fools because they were certain the staff could tell just by looking at them that they'd spent the night together. Esther had also been convinced that they could tell that they'd slept rough, but Kit didn't agree.

'Do we look the type to do wild camping?' he'd asked.

'We didn't have a tent, so it couldn't possibly be classed as camping,' she'd objected, and a lively discussion had followed, only ending when he'd dropped her off at her flat, promising to return at seven. He told her he was going to bring a bottle of wine with him, too.

Did that mean he thought he was going to stay the night (too much to drink equated to not being able to drive) or was he simply being polite and bringing wine to a dinner date at someone's house because that was the accepted thing to do?

There she was again with the second guessing, and she shook the duvet out with considerably more force than the task warranted. She eyed the fresh cover that she'd put on and wrinkled her nose, telling herself that the bed needed changing anyway and not to read too much into it.

As for the rest of her preparations, the candles were pretty and gave off a nice smell, it was about time she shaved her legs and plucked her eyebrows because she was starting to resemble an orangutan, and her hair was overdue for a good dollop of the expensive conditioner that she saved for special occasions. The flat had needed a good clean, and she reasoned that she'd do the same if it was any of her friends coming around for a meal. They could hardly be expected to eat at a dirty table with the floor covered in crumbs and other unrecognisable bits and pieces. Actually, the flat was clean enough already, as she'd found it much easier to keep on top of things since Josh had moved out. She hadn't realised how much picking up after him she'd done, or what a mess he used to make. She knew for a fact that Kit wasn't such a slob; she'd seen first-hand that he was tidy and neat, and knew what an oven was for. He also knew how to wash dishes afterwards, which was a bonus. She couldn't remember Josh ever washing up. She didn't think he knew how…

What was she doing thinking about Josh anyway? Was it because Kit would be the first fella to put a foot over her doorstep since her ex had dumped her? It would actually be a bit strange to see Kit in her flat, sitting where Josh had sat— Hang on, if she moved the furniture around, then the place would look a little different. There were two hours to go before Kit was due to arrive and she had to keep herself occupied somehow, or else she would go out of her mind. She was wound up enough already, the excitement of seeing him later making her heart skip about in her chest as it missed a beat or two.

When she'd finally finished dragging the sofa from one side of the living room to the other, trying to find the best location, in other words one where it wasn't stuck in the middle of the room and where she could still see the TV, and she had pulled and pushed the two armchairs into complementary positions, she needed another shower.

Best make it quick, she thought, checking the time. The food was nearly ready, but she decided she could afford a few minutes, especially since she'd already washed and dried her hair and her clothes were laid out on the bed.

It was while she was drying herself off that she heard the buzzer go and her heart sank. He was early by ten whole minutes!

Wrapping a towel around her chest, she dashed into the hall, pressed the button which opened the downstairs door, then scampered into her bedroom to swiftly get dressed.

'I'll be with you in a second,' she called as she heard footsteps in the hall. 'I'm just putting some clothes on.'

'Don't bother, Essie,' a familiar voice called back and Esther let out a squeak, putting out a hand to steady herself.

No, it can't be… Oh, bloody hell.

She shot into the hall, her fingers fumbling with the buttons of her blouse as she tried to do them up, and came face to face with Josh.

And Kit.

Josh sniffed appreciatively. 'Something smells nice. What are we having, and who's this guy?' He jerked his head at Kit, who was hovering in the doorway, a bottle of wine in one hand and an enormous bouquet in the other.

'Sticky hoisin chicken with rice,' she answered automatically. 'What are you doing here?'

Josh gave her a cocky smile. 'Hang on a sec – it's the downstairs flat you want mate, not this one,' he said to Kit over his shoulder.

Kit was staring at her, his expression one of shock and confusion.

'No, he's got the right flat,' Esther said taking a step towards Kit. Unfortunately, that also meant moving closer to Josh, who took the opportunity to grab her around the waist and pull her towards him.

'Josh, get off.' She tried to push him away, but he was busily nosing at her neck. 'Let me—'

'Stick the flowers on the floor, mate, thanks. It's not your birthday is it?' Josh interrupted, lifting his head for a moment, and she took the opportunity to grab a handful of hair on the back of his head and tug. There was no way she was going to let him slobber all over her neck again. Ew!

'Get off me!' she yelled at him when he failed to take the hint and went in for another clinch, then she saw Kit turn on his heel and march back down the stairs.

'Wait,' she called, trying to twist out of Josh's arms. 'Kit!'

'Kit? Yeah, that's a good idea – get your kit off. I've missed you so much, babe. Can you forgive me?'

It seemed to be a rhetorical question, as Josh kept nibbling at her, not expecting an answer and fully expecting her to say she'd forgive him anything.

'For God's sake Josh, will you sodding well leave me alone?' she screamed, right in his ear.

He jerked back. 'Ow, that hurt. There's no need to shout, babe, I know you're a bit upset with me, but—'

'Upset? *Upset!* Try sodding furious. You really hurt me, you bastard, and now I've—' She heard the downstairs door slam shut and she cringed, tears threatening to spill over. What must Kit be thinking? She should go after him, but she wanted to make sure Josh left first. And she had to make him give the flat keys back.

'Yeah, about that,' Josh was saying. 'Charlie told me you was pining for me.'

'Charlie should learn to keep her mouth shut. And "was" is the operative word. I'm not pining for you any longer.'

'Yeah, you are,' Josh smirked. 'She told me about the webcam.'

'So I noticed, when you snogged every girl you could get your hands on.' A tear trickled down her cheek and she dashed it away with the back of her hand.

'Aww, Essie baby, there's no need to cry. I'm back now.'

'I'm not crying over *you*, you idiot. I'm crying because— never mind, it's none of your business. Just get out. Go.' Suddenly deflated, she sagged against the wall, all the fight having drained out of her. 'Please.'

'But, babe…'

'And don't call me babe. Or Essie. My name is Esther.'

Josh made no move to go, but he did narrow his eyes at her. 'Who was that bloke just now?' he asked slowly, looking around the hall.

Kit had taken the flowers with him.

'My boss – one of them.'

He leered at her, knowingly. 'It's like that, is it?'

'No. It's not.' Her reply was short and uttered through gritted teeth. 'And even if it was, it wouldn't be any of your business. Please, just go. Leave me alone. You don't live here anymore.'

'My name's on the lease.' His smirk was starting to irritate her. How had she ever thought he was sexy?

'Actually, it's not. I had it changed.'

'You can't do that!'

Esther shrugged. 'My landlord seemed to think I can. So, you need to give me my keys and go.' She held her hand out.

The smugness slowly seeped out of Josh's face and he shifted from foot to foot, a sure sign he was feeling uncomfortable. 'My mum's not well,' he said after a long pause.

Esther continued to hold out her hand. 'What's wrong with her?'

'Cancer.'

Her hand dropped down to her side. 'Is it serious?'

He bit his lip. 'I think so. She's not telling.'

Esther shook her head slowly. 'That's why you've come back, because of your mum. Not because of me.' She took a deep breath. 'I'm sorry about Debbie, even though we never saw eye to eye, but you can't stay here. You should be with her.'

'Aw, babes – *Esther* – you know we'd drive each other mad. And she does like you, deep down. I bet she'd appreciate you doing a bit of washing and ironing for her. She'd like that.'

'You astound me. You think you can waltz back into my life and pick up where we left off, just so I can help you look after your mum.' She put her hands on her hips and glared at him. 'No chance. You can learn to use a washing machine and no doubt Debbie will give you lessons in how to iron. I wish your mum all the best, and tell her I'm thinking about her, but you need to give me my keys back and get out.'

Reluctantly he held them out to her and she snatched them from him before he could change his mind. She watched him sidle out of the door as he shot her several hangdog looks. She didn't move and her expression didn't alter.

It was only when she heard the downstairs door close that she slammed the door to the flat shut and sagged against it. He was gone, hopefully for good.

She hoped she couldn't say the same thing about Kit.

With shaking hands, she reached for her phone…

CHAPTER 45

Kit unlocked his car and threw the bouquet of flowers onto the back seat, the bottle of wine quickly following. He got in and started the engine, barely checking that it was safe to pull out before he accelerated away from the kerb.

She'd said her ex was in Spain.

Obviously he wasn't.

The man had sauntered into the building and up the stairs as though he lived there, and maybe he still did because he still had a set of keys.

Josh had followed Kit through the door after Kit had pressed the buzzer, and he'd assumed the man was heading to the first floor flat. Josh had squeezed past him with a vague 'All right, mate?' and had trotted up the stairs ahead of him, taking them two at a time. Kit had walked up behind him and had blinked in surprise when the guy had continued up to the second floor and had used a key to open the door to Esther's flat.

It didn't take him long to realise that the guy must be Esther's ex-boyfriend, and from the way he was behaving, that he didn't consider himself to be that much of an ex.

Briefly Kit had wondered if he should stay…

He'd soon changed his mind when the man had assumed he was from Interflora. The possibility that Esther might be seeing someone didn't appear to have entered the bloke's mind, making Kit think that maybe Josh wasn't as much of an ex as Esther had led him to believe.

Christ, what a mess – both of them embroiled in other relationships (although, to be fair, Kit was desperately trying to extricate himself from his) yet they'd spent the most magical night together last night. He hadn't imagined that she'd enjoyed it as much as he had. Or had he?

Having Josh turn up on her doorstep when she thought he was still in Spain must have been quite a shock for her.

It had been a damned shock to him too.

He thought of the look on her face when she'd seen the pair of them, and he wasn't sure what he'd seen. Dismay? Guilt? Embarrassment?

He tried to think, but his thoughts were jumbled

and chaotic. All that stood out was that Esther hadn't hesitated in stepping straight into Josh's arms as the man had caught her around the waist and pulled her towards him. She'd even grabbed the back of the guy's head, and he'd thought they were going to start kissing, but she'd told Josh to get off and he guessed she hadn't wanted an audience.

He drove back to the cottage, the journey barely registering, and it was only when he pulled into the drive and yanked the handbrake on that the full force of what had happened hit him.

Her betrayal was like a knife to his heart, slicing deep, and the pain of it surged through him.

Stop being so ridiculous, he said to himself. He hardly knew the woman, and they'd only shared a few kisses (OK, more than a few). But last night had only been their third date; their relationship had barely begun. They'd not declared their undying love for one another. It wasn't even as if they'd been seeing each other for months. Three dates. Three!

So why was he so cut up about her ex (not so ex) coming back on the scene?

He should be chalking it up to experience, shrugging it off and walking away, not wallowing in misery and feeling as though his whole world had come crashing down. In the space of a few minutes he'd gone from deliriously happy and being filled with excited anticipation, to feeling as though he'd lost the only thing in his life worth living for. Christ, he hadn't felt this bad when Nancy had announced she was leaving him.

He closed his eyes and groaned in dismay. Did this mean what he thought it meant?

Surely not. He couldn't have fallen in love with Esther in such a short space of time and without realising it, *could he*?

His phone rang and he withdrew it from the pocket of his jeans.

Esther.

His heart lurched when he saw her name.

He didn't answer it. Instead, he turned his phone off and replaced it slowly. He didn't want to hear her excuses, her explanation. Whatever she said to him wasn't going to alter what had just happened.

It was a damned pity she worked for him though, because he'd still have to have some contact with her. For the time being. Although if his plans came to fruition, then he shortly wouldn't have to have anything to do with her at all.

But that didn't stop him from feeling as though his heart had been torn from his chest, stomped on, and put back in.

He should have listened to his head, not his heart and not allowed himself to get involved with her. It was too soon after Nancy and, he recalled bitterly, he'd vowed not to bother with the opposite sex for a very long time, if ever. He should have stuck to his vow. Now look at him, and he only had himself to blame for having his heart broken.

Stupid, stupid, stupid…

CHAPTER 46

Esther seriously didn't want to go into work today. Or ever again. Not with the prospect of bumping into Kit, or the risk of him being on the other end of the phone when she answered it. Or seeing anything with his name on, or driving past Wildflower Lane and knowing he might be in his cottage, or… Anything that might bring a fresh wave of pain, really.

She knew she looked dreadful, having not slept at all last night. After the fifth attempt she'd given up trying to phone him. Kit obviously hadn't been that into her, and had most likely agreed to have dinner at her place because there had been the (very real) possibility of getting her into bed.

Josh turning up must have proved to be more of a complication than Kit was prepared to handle just for a quick fumble between the sheets. Baggage, that's what he must have seen Josh as, and he'd decided to get out now before things became too complicated. With her ex back on the scene and trying to get back with her, Kit had cut his losses. And she didn't blame him. She'd have probably done the same thing if the shoe was on the other foot. What if that woman who she'd seen in his cottage turned up and was all over him? She'd probably bow out and leave the pair of them to it, rather than risk getting caught in the middle of something.

Anyway, it was her own fault that she was hurting as much as she was – they'd had a couple of dates and shared some kisses. She couldn't blame him for the fact that she'd read more into it than had been there. On his part, at least. Their relationship had been so new and so tender that it was no surprise it hadn't stood up to Josh barging in and expecting to take up where he'd left off. He'd made his intentions pretty clear and although she thought she'd also made her rebuffal of him crystal clear, it was obviously more hassle than Kit was prepared to deal with.

She stared at her reflection in the staff loo, wincing at the sight of the bags under her eyes and the purple shadows around them. She looked pale and slightly ill. Her face being devoid of makeup didn't help, but she simply hadn't had the energy to make the effort this morning. Her hair was in the messiest of messy buns, and she looked as though she'd got dressed in the dark.

She didn't care. Dean would have to take her or leave her – he was lucky she'd managed to make it into work at all. Exhaustion, both physical and emotional, gripped her, making her feel dull and lethargic, and somewhat unwell.

However, she realised that staying off work wasn't an option, not if she wanted to carry on working at LandScape Ltd, and she very much did want that. Despite Kit and the situation she'd landed herself in, she loved her job and would hate to give it up, especially when there was no need to.

The next time she saw Kit she'd calmly explain what had happened and offer her apologies, and if she was professional and polite about it, then they could both move on from there, put it behind them and resume their working relationship. There was no need for her to quit – as long as she could contain her desolation, and she was sure she could. Eventually she'd get over Kit and life would carry on as it had before. After all, he didn't know how she felt about him, apart from suspecting she liked him. He wasn't to know that her feelings ran much deeper than that. Aloof and distant, that's what she'd be, and before long she'd be totally over him.

She hoped.

At least she had work to take her mind off things

(to a degree), and anything was better than sitting in her flat and crying. She'd done enough of that last night. So she threw herself into her job and tried to block him from her mind, which was easier said than done, but she managed it for several whole minutes at one point.

LandScape had landed a major contract to design all the grounds of a new head office for a well-known and prestigious company, and Esther wanted to finish typing up the order of works for final approval before she went home. Or that's what she was telling herself. She should have left half an hour ago but the end of the document was in sight and besides, she only had last night's sticky chicken and an empty flat to go home to. She most definitely wasn't working late in the hope that Kit, assuming she'd left for the day, would show his face.

When she heard a car pull up outside, her tummy turned over. Shit, she couldn't do this, she should have left earlier. Feeling sick, she heard a car door slam, followed by footsteps on the gravel, then the click of heels on the path.

The door handle turned.

Esther kept her eyes firmly on her computer screen, trying to appear absorbed in her work but guessing she probably wasn't fooling anyone.

The door opened.

Esther swallowed convulsively.

Unable to help herself, she looked up.

It wasn't Kit. It was a woman, about the same age as her, she guessed, but considerably more polished. She oozed sophistication, and every part of her, from the top of her shining head to the toes of her incredibly high heeled shoes, screamed high maintenance.

Esther noticed all this in one swift scan and she felt positively dowdy, scruffy and plain in comparison.

I bet she owns a massive house, she thought, with a swimming pool and a gym, and maybe her own cinema. The woman looked like something out of House and Garden, and she wondered what her name was and what LandScape was doing for her. Whatever it was, it was probably extensive and expensive. She'd seen what LandScape Ltd charged!

'Can I help you?' Esther asked in her poshest voice as the woman made to walk straight past her, heading towards Dean's office. She'd clearly been here before.

The woman stopped and swivelled on her heels to stare at her. 'And you are…?'

'Esther. Do you have an appointment?'

'I don't need one.'

Oh, right.' She picked up the phone. 'I'll let Mr Reynolds know you're here, if you'd like to take a seat.' She gestured towards the seating area.

'No thanks, I'll go straight in. And for future reference, I'm Kit's wife, Nancy Reynolds.'

Esther froze, her fingers hovering above the buttons.

For a second, she wasn't certain she heard correctly, but when the woman stalked into Dean's office she heard him say, 'Nancy. This is a surprise. Does Kit know you're here?' before the door clicked firmly shut behind her.

Wife?

She'd said *wife.*

What the…?

Esther slowly replaced the receiver, and slumped back in her chair.

He had a wife?

She didn't believe it. He'd never have kissed her if he had…

Or maybe he would have. What did she really know about him? Obviously not a lot, if she wasn't aware of a wife.

And what a wife Nancy was. Glamorous didn't go halfway to describing her, so what was Kit doing playing around with someone like Esther? She was under no illusions about herself – she was pretty enough, in a girl next door kind of way, but she wasn't in the same league as his wife. She wasn't sure she was even on the same planet.

Fresh pain ripped through her, as she thought about the way he'd kissed her – as though she was the only woman in the world who mattered, and she wondered what excuse he'd given for not going home the other night? Maybe that's why Nancy Reynolds was here now, to ask if Dean knew anything about it?

She didn't bother saving the document she'd been working so assiduously on. She didn't bother turning her computer off, either. She simply grabbed her bag and walked out.

It wasn't easy waiting until she got home before letting the hot, heavy tears fall, but she managed to stagger in through the door and kick it shut behind her before she broke down and sobbed her heart out.

God, she felt such a fool. And to think she'd fallen for him.

She'd *have* to leave LandScape Ltd now. How could she stay there after this?

The thought of seeing Kit again filled her with such sadness that she didn't think she could bear it. She'd hand her resignation in tomorrow. She had to give Dean a month's notice and she intended to work it, despite knowing that it would be unbearable. She owed him that much – it wasn't his fault that his brother was a two-timing, unfaithful bastard.

And what hurt nearly as much was the knowledge that she only had herself to blame. If she'd stuck to her principles and hadn't got involved with someone at work, then she wouldn't be in this awful predicament.

She was back to square one – actually she was worse off. Not only did she not have a boyfriend, but she was having to give up a job she loved, and she'd have to go crawling back to the agency and beg them to take her back.

What a mess her life was turning out to be.

CHAPTER 47

'What are you doing here?' Kit asked as he opened his front door to see his brother standing on the other side of it.

'Funnily enough, I've not long ago said the exact same thing to your wife.' Dean pushed past him and strode into the living room. 'When were you going to tell me?'

Kit sighed. 'Tomorrow. I only found out myself today.'

'And you decided that Nancy should be the first person to know, and not me? I'm the person who'll be the most affected.'

'It wasn't like that.' He dropped wearily into a chair. It had been one hell of a twenty-four hours.

'What *was* it like?' Dean remained standing, towering over him like a vengeful angel of death. Kit had the impression that Dean wanted to do more than kill him right now.

'I told Nash Layton, who must have informed Nancy's solicitor straight away,' he explained.

'She came to the office and took great delight in telling me that she now owns half of LandScape. Half! I thought a quarter was bad enough, but *half*.'

Kit rubbed a hand over his chin, feeling the rasp of stubble on his palm. 'That's not what's going to happen. She's got the wrong end of the stick. Either that, or she wants to cause one last bit of trouble.'

'You'd better tell me what's going to happen then, because she seemed pretty adamant.'

'I've informed Nash that I'm sacrificing my share of LandScape Ltd in order to buy Nancy out of her half of the cottage. I can't lose my home, Dean, I simply can't.'

'You're putting *your* cottage before *our* business? I don't believe it.'

'Not exactly. Yes, I'm selling my share and no, I know you can't raise the funds to cover it. But Dad can.'

'*Dad?* How?'

'It turns out he owns that field behind my house and the two adjacent to it.'

'I never knew that.' Dean finally took a seat. He was perched uneasily on the edge of it, but it was a start.

'Neither did I, until recently. He'd been renting it out for years to Amos Brinkman, but I only found out about it when I went to see Amos about a webcam.'

'I don't follow.'

'Esther told me that there was a camera trained on the back of my house and anyone with internet access could view it. Amos had installed it when he had those mares in the field and had forgotten to switch it off. It had turned itself around somehow, probably when we had that storm back in April, and was showing my living room and kitchen to anyone who cared to look.'

'Crikey!'

'Exactly. Anyway, when I asked him to take it down, he told me he was renting the fields and that he'd been begging Dad for years to sell them to him, but Dad had always said no. It gave me an idea, so I went to see Mum and Dad last week. They said they knew that neither of us had any interest in farming, and said they might as well sell some of the land now as sell it later when they were too old to manage the farm any longer. Dad spoke to Amos and they agreed a fair price, and my solicitor is currently drawing up the documents to transfer my share of the business into Dad's name. With the money from the sale, I can give Nancy a decent sum.'

'But I thought a settlement would have to be made by the courts?'

'I did, too. But if an agreement can be reached out of court, then it's better for both parties. I, for one, seriously didn't want to pay a solicitor any more than I had to.'

'I can't believe she agreed.'

'I can. Nash gave me a guestimate of how much she owed and told me she'd been ignoring her solicitor's advice that she wouldn't get as much as she thought she'd get if it went to court. It seemed like she's finally seen sense. It helped matters that my offer was generous.'

'Thank God for that, although why she felt the need to stir up trouble, I don't know,' Dean said. Then he added, shrewdly, 'Not too generous, I hope?'

Kit gave his brother a wan smile.

Dean studied him. 'It is, isn't it? I hope you know what you're doing, because—'

'It's not that.'

'What is it?'

'Esther.'

Dean frowned. 'What about her?'

'I know you're going to tear a strip off me, and believe me I deserve it, but I've been on a couple of dates with her.'

'And?' He was still scrutinising him, and Kit

grimaced.

'I've fallen for her and thought she was beginning to have feelings for me. But her ex turned up yesterday evening and it looks like they've picked up where they left off.'

Dean puffed out his cheeks, then shook his head. 'She doesn't look deliriously happy about it, if she is back with her ex. She looked a bit upset, actually.'

'She did?' Kit's heart lifted a fraction. Maybe, just maybe…?

'Tell me what happened.'

'She invited me to hers for a meal, but when I arrived her ex showed up at the same time.' He barked out a short bitter laugh. 'He thought I was the guy from Interflora. Anyway, she went straight into his arms and I left.'

'You didn't give her a chance to explain?'

'I didn't need to – it was obvious.'

'Has she tried to contact you? Or you, her?'

Kit shook his head, then stopped. 'She did try to call me, but I ignored her.'

'You should let her tell you her side of the story. It might not be what you think. Anyway, you've got to keep working with her, so it'll be good to clear the air. And next time, please keep your work life and your personal life separate because nothing good ever comes of mixing the two.'

'Yeah, you're right. I'll pop in and speak to her tomorrow. I don't want there to be any awkwardness.' It wasn't fair on Dean to have to work in that kind of an atmosphere.

Dean chuckled. 'You do realise that once the sale is finalised, I'll be your boss? Don't worry, I'll be a fair one.' He slapped his hand on his thigh and Kit narrowed his eyes at him.

Dean being his employer wasn't something he relished, and he might never have considered selling his share of LandScape but for one thing.

'Er… about that… I've, um, got something else to tell you….'

CHAPTER 48

'You've got a nerve,' Kit said when he opened the door to see Nancy standing there. 'What the hell are you playing at? I can't believe you went to see my brother.'

'Hello, Kit, lovely to see you too,' Nancy said. 'Can I come in?'

Kit was in two minds to tell her where to go, or make her say what she had to say while standing on the doorstep, but he didn't want any neighbours wandering past and hearing something he'd prefer to keep private. So he opened the door wider and stood to one side.

'Well?' he demanded, following her into the living room. The way she'd walked into his house as though she had a right to be there, with a hip-swaying swaggering confidence, seriously got his back up. And he was relieved to see that the sight of her no longer had any effect on him.

She was still remarkably beautiful and her dress sense was second to none, but he couldn't help comparing her to Esther's natural prettiness. The two women were worlds apart. Nancy reminded him of an airbrushed photo in a glossy magazine, whereas Esther was a crazy snap taken with friends, full of life and laughter. He knew which he preferred.

'That's not very friendly,' Nancy said, her perfect lips forming a seductive pout.

'Give it a rest,' he muttered, then louder, 'What do you want?'

'I would never have thought you'd choose this house over your brother and your business,' she said. 'But I suppose you always did like the country life.' The way she said it made it sound like she'd scraped something off the bottom of her shoe.

Kit refused to be drawn. He had nothing to say to her and there was nothing she could say to him that he wanted to hear. They were done. Over. Finished.

But then Nancy, he'd come to realise, didn't like letting go, even when Kit had served his purpose and was no longer useful to her. She'd got what she wanted from him (enough money to keep her happy – for a while), but she couldn't resist a final turn of the knife.

What she didn't understand was that the knife was

blunt and she was no longer able to hurt him. The only thing he felt for her now was a sense of pity and a vague regret for what might have been if things had been different.

‘I know about her,’ Nancy said. ‘Your new woman.’

Kit raised his eyes. It wasn’t a secret but it was hardly common knowledge either.

‘Admittedly, she does look more your type. Earthy and rural.’ Nancy spat the last few words out with venom.

Ah, so that’s what the visit to Dean had been about. She’d been trying to cause trouble because she was jealous. Not that she wanted him herself. She just didn’t want anyone else to have him.

‘Yes, she is,’ he agreed, ‘and that’s one of the things I love about her ’ He stopped and his heart leapt into his throat. Did he just say what he thought he’d said? And if so, did he mean it?

Nancy narrowed her eyes at him, her chin jutting out as her face hardened. ‘It didn’t take you long, did it?’ she sneered.

Kit took a steadying breath. ‘Do I need to remind you that you were the one who walked out on our marriage? You were the one who wanted a divorce, not me. We could have been happy, Nancy, but you threw it all away. Now, if you’ll excuse me, I’ve got things to do.' He gestured to the hall.

Nancy hesitated for a second, then seemed to gather herself together. She lifted her chin, stuck her pert nose in the air and stalked out of his house and out of his life, and this time Kit knew he'd seen the last of her.

He was finally free of her. Free to live his life as he wanted. Free to find love again.

Although, to him it did look like he'd already found it.

He only hoped that the woman he loved felt the same way.

CHAPTER 49

Esther had suffered another fitful night and wasn't in the best of moods. She'd tossed and turned, mulling over and over in her mind the fact that Kit had a wife, until she'd almost driven herself to distraction. There was something else bothering her, too. The woman she'd seen on the webcam wasn't the same woman who said she was his wife. Was he a serial adulterer? Was Esther one in a long list of women he'd been unfaithful with? She had a horrid suspicion that she might be.

In the end, she'd got up, made a cup of tea and had typed her resignation.

Before she had a chance to change her mind or second guess herself, she'd attached it to an email and sent it to Dean. She'd addressed it to both the brothers but assumed that Kit probably wouldn't get to see it, or if he did, he wouldn't care. Why would he when he had a *wife*?

It may cross his mind that Esther might tell Nancy that her husband had been playing around (it had crossed Esther's too, during the course of the long, lonely night, but she wasn't that vindictive) and he might try to speak to her to persuade her to keep her mouth shut, but she had a feeling he wasn't too concerned about being caught. If he was worried that his wife would find out, then he wouldn't have taken risks so close to home, so to speak.

Esther wondered if Kit and Nancy had one of those open marriages, and she shuddered with distaste.

Hopefully, she wouldn't have to see him again before she left. No doubt he'd want to keep his distance too, after the other night.

But the following morning, she was utterly shocked to find Kit waiting for her when she walked into LandScape Ltd at her usual time. He was perched on the edge of her desk, one foot on the floor, the other swinging. There were two cups of coffee next to him.

He picked one up and gave it to her.

'Thanks.' She took it cautiously and had a sip. It wasn't as hot as she'd been expecting – how long had he been waiting for her to arrive?

'You look tired,' he said.

'Thanks,' she repeated, sarcastically.

'Dean told me you've handed in your resignation. Is it because of me?'

Esther didn't answer.

'Or because of your boyfriend?'

'What boyfriend?'

'Josh.'

'He's not my boyfriend.'

'You could have fooled me.'

'The way *you* fooled *me*?'

'Pardon?'

'I know about Nancy.'

He grimaced and took a deep breath. 'Ah, I see, I should have told you from the start, but I didn't want to scare you off.'

'Really?'

'Yeah…'

'How could you! I was starting to— Never mind. I'll work my months' notice but you'd better advertise for my replacement now.'

'You and Josh aren't together?'

'No. Not that it's any of your business.' Why was he keeping on about that? It wasn't relevant, not in the light of him being married.

'I'd like to make it my business.'

'You've got to be joking! Piss off back to your wife, you two-timing git. And do you know what? I don't think I will work my notice after all. I don't think I can stand to be in the same building as a man who cheats.'

Esther slammed her coffee down on the desk and whirled on her heel, storming towards the door. What a complete and utter bastard. She couldn't get over his bare-faced cheek. To think that he—

Kit raced after her and he was so close she could feel his warm breath on the back of her neck as he hissed, 'I've *not* been unfaithful. Nancy and I are getting a divorce.'

She stopped abruptly and he crashed into her, nearly knocking her off her feet, before putting his hands out to steady her. She wobbled for a second then regained her balance, and he released her.

'Say that again.' She stared up at him, a flicker of hope igniting in her heart.

'We are getting a divorce,' he repeated. 'I thought you said you knew about Nancy?'

'I thought I did…' Esther took a steadying breath. 'She turned up here yesterday evening to speak to Dean and she introduced herself as your wife.' Introduced sounded much more polite than Nancy had actually been.

'I suppose she still is, technically. Though not for much longer. We've been separated for months. If she hadn't been so greedy, the divorce would have been finalised before I met you, and we wouldn't be having this conversation.'

'I see. You still should have told me. I told you about Josh and we'd broken it off completely. You still have some ties to her.'

'As I said, not for much longer. I was going to tell you when it was all over and done with. I'm sorry, I should have been honest with you from the start.'

'Yes, you should have. There's something else.'

'What?'

'I saw you with another woman, she was at your house.'

'At my house…?' There hadn't been any other women inside his front door since Nancy walked out, except for his mum and Angie. 'You must mean Angie,' he said. 'She's one of my oldest friends and lives in California. She came to visit a few weeks ago, but she's returned home. You must believe me when I say there's absolutely nothing going on between us.'

Esther breathed out a sigh. 'I'm glad,' she said.

'Does that mean you'll stay?'

'I don't think so.'

His face fell, and Esther bit her lip. 'I'm going to be honest with you,' she began. 'One of us has to be. I've fallen for you, and because of that I'm not prepared to continue to work here. Hear me out,' she said, as Kit opened his mouth to speak. 'Having a relationship with someone at work is silly – I think we've just proved that. So if you're here to rekindle our relationship – and I hope you are – then I need to find a job somewhere else.'

There, she'd said it. She'd laid her cards on the table and told him how she felt. Almost. He didn't need to know the full extent of it. The fact that she thought she might be in love with him was something that could be shared at a later date.

'There's no need for you to resign,' he told her, and that little flicker of hope gave a tiny moan of anguish, rolled over and died. She knew exactly what he meant, and her heart ached anew.

At least he'd reinforced her gut feeling that she was doing the right thing by handing in her notice. If he'd said he wanted to see her again, then she would have to leave anyway.

The fact that he didn't also meant that she had to leave, because there was no way she wanted to torture herself by continuing to work here and run the risk of bumping into him on a regular basis. She didn't need that kind of heartache in her life.

'Esther look at me,' he urged.

She looked and what she saw in his eyes made her gasp – they were brimming with love.

'You don't need to resign, because I've sold my share of the business. I'll no longer be your employer.'

'You won't?'

He held out his arms and, after a moment, Esther stepped into them. As he wrapped them around her, she felt like she was coming home.

'No, I won't,' he said. 'I've been offered a job with the Wildlife Trust to head a campaign to encourage people to dedicate a part of their garden or property to wildlife.' He grinned, and she noticed a dimple in his left cheek. Why hadn't she noticed that before? There was so much to be discovered about him…

'My expertise is in the habitat and the planting. I'll visit homes, councils and businesses and plan out their spaces for them, no matter how big or small. I'll be working closely with schools, too.' He took a breath and Esther jumped in.

'What about Dean and LandScape? Who've you sold your half to?' She had an awful feeling Dean mightn't be as delighted with what Kit had done, even if it was the best thing for Kit.

'Our dad. The business is still in the family! Isn't that wonderful? And I've agreed to remain involved by doing freelance work. But enough of all this work talk, I'm more interested in you and me.' He bent his head toward her, but as his lips drew nearer she wriggled out of his arms.

'There's something I need to do first,' she told

him, seeing his face fall. 'Stay there, I won't be long.'

She dashed over to her desk, relieved to see that her computer was still on and she didn't have to wait for it to start. The sooner she retracted her resignation, the sooner she would be back in Kit's arms being kissed by him.

Her fingers flew over the keys, then she pressed send and straightened up.

Kit had remained exactly where he was and she walked slowly over to him. Her lips parted and a blush crept into her cheeks. Warmth tingled through her, washing every cell with happiness.

It might be too early to tell where their relationship would end up, but she had a really good feeling about it.

If the expression on his face was anything to go by, so did Kit.

She stepped into his embrace, his strong arms folding around her, holding her as though he'd never let her go.

And when he kissed her, she knew that this was where she wanted to spend the rest of her life

CHAPTER 50

The meadow behind the cottage on Wildflower Lane was once again dancing with flowers and long grasses waving in the warm summer breeze. The scent of them mingled with freshly mown grass and Esther leant out of the open window and breathed deeply. If the perfume of heaven could be bottled, she thought, it would smell exactly like this.

The day promised to be a glorious one, which was just as well considering it was a very special day indeed. By the end of it, she would be Esther Reynolds. Her heart did that funny little skipped-beat thing whenever she thought about it. She was about to marry the most wonderful man in the world, in the most beautiful place in the world and she was so happy she could cry. Since she'd moved into the cottage last year, she'd fallen a little more in love with it every day (just as she'd done with the man who lived in it), so it seemed only natural that when he'd proposed to her, she'd suggested asking Amos if he'd let them hold the ceremony in his field.

To their delight he'd agreed, and he'd even offered to reinstall the camera so the event could be filmed. He did say he'd make sure it was aimed in the right direction this time!

From the cottage's bedroom window she had a clear view of the field and the billowing white marquee sitting in the middle of it. The sides had been drawn back to allow the outside to spill into the enormous tent, and she caught glimpses of tables and flowers and shining crystal glasses.

The guests were arriving and she should be making her way downstairs soon, but she'd sent Charlie, Sinead, and Amy down ahead of her, wanting a few minutes alone to compose herself.

For quite some time after his divorce had come through, she and Kit had taken their relationship slowly, neither of them wanting to dive straight into a full-blown commitment. They'd taken time to get to know one another properly, to understand one another, and to fall completely and utterly in love. After a while, it seemed only natural that she moved in with him, and then after a few more months, agree to be his bride.

Smoothing her hands down the fine organza of

her skirt, she almost squealed with joy at the thought of the ceremony to come.

Her bouquet was waiting for her on the dressing table, and she stroked the delicate blooms with her fingertips before she picked it up. Composed of a wonderfully chaotic assortment of wildflowers (naturally), Esther could now name every single one. She could name a lot of other plants, too, and she knew whether they thrived best in shade or full sun, whether they liked damp roots or dry soil. She'd learnt an incredible amount since she'd first set foot through the door of LandScape Ltd a little over a year ago, and she'd enjoyed every single moment. Even those moments where she had to deal with difficult customers. Mostly.

Kit, combining his love of wildflowers and wildlife with his love of garden design, was himself flourishing. And although he still took on a considerable number of commissions from Dean, Esther thought there was one obvious advantage to him not having a share in the business – they didn't work together. But he did enjoy hearing her stories and being involved in LandScape Ltd through her.

She glanced out of the window again. There was Kit's friend, Angie, home for their wedding and Esther adored her already. They were planning a trip to California next spring, when they were hoping there would be a bloom of wildflowers for them to see.

Leaning out again, she spotted Kit and Dean's parents entering the marquee, and she felt a rush of affection for the elderly couple. They'd embraced her into the family with open arms, treating her like a daughter – which was something they'd never done with Nancy, apparently. Thankfully Kit's ex-wife was well and truly out of their lives and out of the country, having moved to America. Esther had no idea what the woman was doing over there, but she hoped she was being successful at it and would stay there. Just like Josh would stay in Malaga, where he'd returned shortly after his mum was told that the lump she'd found wasn't malignant. Unsurprisingly enough, Esther hadn't had the slightest urge to sneak a look at Flamingo Cam…

She had, however, spent a great deal of time watching a pretty little square in a seaside town in Italy where she and Kit were about to jet off to tomorrow on their honeymoon. Eek! She couldn't wait!

Taking one last look out of the window at the glorious scene before her, Esther's gaze was drawn to Kit, who hovered outside the marquee with Dean as best man by his side, and she knew that she'd found the love of her life. Her heart sang and her spirits soared, and she firmly believed she must be the luckiest woman in the world.

ABOUT THE AUTHOR

Liz Davies writes feel-good, light-hearted stories with a hefty dose of romance, a smattering of humour, and a great deal of love.

She's married to her best friend, has one grown-up daughter, and when she isn't scribbling away in the notepad she carries with her everywhere (just in case inspiration strikes), you'll find her searching for that perfect pair of shoes. She loves to cook but isn't very good at it, and loves to eat - she's much better at that! Liz also enjoys walking (preferably on the flat), cycling (also on the flat), and lots of sitting around in the garden on warm, sunny days.

She currently lives with her family in Wales, but would ideally love to buy a camper van and travel the world in it.

Social Media Links:
Twitter https://twitter.com/lizdaviesauthor
Facebook: fb.me/LizDaviesAuthor1

Printed in Great Britain
by Amazon